# ROAD TRIP: BBQ AND A BRAWL

# ROAD TRIP: BBQ AND A BRAWL

## THE UNBELIEVABLE MR. BROWNSTONE™ BOOK NINETEEN

## MICHAEL ANDERLE

DISRUPTIVE IMAGINATION®

Copyright © 2019 Michael Anderle
Cover by Andrew Dobell, www.creativeedgestudios.co.uk
Cover copyright © LMBPN Publishing
A Michael Anderle Production

LMBPN Publishing
PMB 196, 2540 South Maryland Pkwy
Las Vegas, NV 89109

First US edition, May 2019
ISBN: 978-1-64202-316-9
Version 1.05, December 2019

**Special Thanks**
to Mike Ross
for BBQ Consulting
Jessie Rae's BBQ - Las Vegas, NV

**Thanks to the JIT Readers**

Daniel Weigert
Nicole Emens
Dave Hicks
Diane L. Smith
Peter Manis
Jeff Eaton
Jeff Goode
James Caplan
Shari Regan
Larry Omans
Paul Westman
Dorothy Lloyd
Micky Cocker

*If I've missed anyone, please let me know!*

**Editor**
Lynne Stiegler

*To Family, Friends and
Those Who Love
to Read.
May We All Enjoy Grace
to Live the Life We Are
Called.*

CHAPTER ONE

J ames paced his living room, Thomas barking at his
    heels. The dog wagged his tail happily, apparently
    under the impression this was a fun new game rather
than a reflection of his master's lingering concerns about
the new complexities coming into his life.

A man who had defeated five Vax living weapons of
mass destruction eight years prior and still managed to
capture—or kill—a level four or five once a year had been
confronted by a problem he couldn't solve through the
massive application of force or a few explosions.

The whole situation was disconcerting, if not irritating.
James had long since given up on life being simple, but that
didn't stop him from growing uncomfortable when it got
more complicated than normal, even when the reasons
were a blessing.

*A kid's a kid. I can't order them around for a few years.
That's gonna be interesting. I wonder if Whispy can change me
so I'll need less sleep?*

Shay rolled her eyes. She sat on the couch, her legs crossed. "You're doing it again, James. And it's really damned annoying. Cut it out."

James stopped, grunted, and turned toward his wife. "Doing what? I'm not doing shit. I'm just…walking. A man can't walk in his living room?"

Shay flicked her wrist. "You're pacing like a high school girl convinced her boyfriend's not going to ask her to prom." She clucked her tongue. "And like I said, it's annoying."

James stared at his wife, the wheels of his mind grinding on the simile. "I was just thinking about shit. It's not a big deal."

Shay patted her stomach. "You mean you were thinking about the kid who's gonna pop out in July and how it's going to be complicated, and you don't know how you'll handle it because you can't just armor up and threaten the baby to get what you want?"

James nodded slowly. He wandered over to his recliner to take a seat. "Yeah. Well, not the part where I threaten the baby."

Thomas barked once before settling beside the chair. He dropped his head between his paws.

James glanced down at the dog. Thomas grew a little grayer around the muzzle with each passing year. James had never been a hundred percent sure how old Thomas was when he found him, but Thomas remained pretty damned spry for a dog who was likely a minimum of ten years old, if not older.

*I hope he lives long enough for my kid to appreciate him. I can get a new dog, but it won't be the same. Just like Thomas wasn't the same as Leeroy.*

Thomas' change also reminded James that his features had scarcely changed in years, leaving little hint that he was eight solid years into his basic retirement. Whispy had idly mentioned "increased basal mitochondrial and whole-cell regeneration" and implied that meant James would live longer than a normal human. James interpreted that as the symbiont admitting to making longevity modifications to his body, but Shay had barely visibly aged a day either, and she hadn't mentioned using any magic or artifacts, so maybe the symbiont was just screwing with him. He wouldn't put it past Whispy.

"It's like you said. It's just complicated." James shrugged. "There's a lot to think about and do. Babies aren't like restaurants, bounty hunts, or tomb raids."

"Sure, but we don't have to get everything figured out for the next eighteen years right away."

"We need to get the birth shit figured out."

Shay snorted. "It's not our wedding, James. It doesn't have to be some fucking epic birth. We don't need an Air Force overflight and big magic displays. We're sitting on enough money to drown a whole city of leprechauns, and no one has the balls to target us anymore. I'll just go to the hospital when it's time and have the kid."

"Not saying any of that." James furrowed his brow. "But the baby might be different. Even if I show up as human on DNA tests, there's obviously DNA crap their tests can't detect. That doesn't bother you at all? You're not worried even a little bit?"

"Nope. You were human enough to knock me up. I'm

3

not worried." Shay laughed. "The way you're carrying on, you'd think you were the one who had to carry this baby. Is that a Vax thing?" She frowned, suddenly looking unsure. "You never mentioned it before if it is."

James shook his head. "Not that I know of. I'm just saying the baby's going to change things, and I have a few other worries. Nothing more than that."

Shay held up a hand. "Look, I get it. Grill or kill it, that's the James Brownstone way, but we did fine with Alison, so I don't think adding a few years on the front end is going to mess things up. We've got the life experience and resources to handle this kid, and I'm not worried at all about the baby's health. If anything, it'll just be stronger and tougher than a normal kid. That's not a bad thing."

James scratched behind Thomas' ears. "Yeah, I guess so. I've just been listening to baby podcasts, and they've been filling my head with ideas. Lots of shit to keep track of. You know, we'll probably have to say things like 'shit' less. It'll be weird."

"That's bothering you?"

"Not *bothering* me. It's just something I'm thinking about."

Shay cackled. "Is that gonna be a problem? Sure, I like a nice curse word or hundred, but it's not like when I lecture at the university, I can say, 'Okay, listen up, you dumb fucks. Midterms are coming, and I've fucking laid out everything you need on the damned syllabus.'" She shook her head. "You spend too much time hiding in the back at your restaurant instead of dealing with customers. The world's mightiest bounty hunter, and now the world's best pitmaster, but damned if you're not still terrible with most people."

"Not saying I can't control my mouth. I'm just saying it's something we'll need to worry about, is all." James shrugged. "And I like cooking barbeque, not talking to people. I didn't open a restaurant because I wanted to chat with customers. Mack and the rest of the staff are better at that kind of thing, and they actually like it."

"Fair enough," Shay agreed. "I forgot to tell you—speaking of Brownstone kids, I talked to Alison yesterday."

James frowned. "Is everything okay? From what I was told by Johnston and a few others there weren't gonna be any problems with the Canadian government or ours. I thought the Canadians even said it basically would count as a bounty situation. If they're trying to start some shit now, they're gonna be really sorry." He let out a loud growl.

Shay shook her head. "No, no. No problems with the government, ours or theirs. You didn't even go full Forerunner, so technically you didn't violate your agreement, even if you and Alison broke a few laws by just popping over there without filing the appropriate paperwork first." A wicked grin spread over her face. "And even if you did go full-out, I don't know if they'd care. You went Forerunner for that Chile thing earlier this year, and no one ended up bitching. Hell, the Chilean government wanted to give you a medal. I guess it's convenient when you take care of major problems for them."

"If it's not a government, then what's the problem?" James narrowed his eyes. "Did those dark wizard fucks not get the message? Because I'm fine with letting Mack handle shit at the restaurant if we need to bring more pain to those assholes. If taking down one of their bases didn't make it clear, we'll just keep going until they get it. Eventually, they'll run out of people, just like the Harriken. I don't care if a few roaches survive."

Shay waved a hand. "Calm down. We don't need to kill anyone else. Alison told me dark wizard factions are falling all over themselves to explain that they'll never mess with her again, that the Seventh Order was a 'rogue faction,' and shit like that." She snickered. "I think just whispering 'Brownstone' near them makes them wet their pants, and hell, Berens too. The dark wizards get that screwing with her is just going to end up with more of them dead." She smiled. "No, she mostly was just checking in. I think she's just dealing with some of the emotional aftermath, but she's got good people up there, including her boyfriend." She sighed. "I'm still annoyed that I couldn't help. Maybe I should have gone up there anyway. As long as I didn't take a serious hit, it wouldn't have been a risk, but then again, it sounds like there were enough people kicking ass even without me."

"It was a good crew." James nodded. "Everyone did their part, so Alison and Izzie could do what they needed to do to end the crap."

"There was one thing Alison asked about that I didn't have a good answer for, and now is as good as time as any to talk about them." Shay folded her hands on her lap and leaned back against the couch. "Baby names."

"Huh?"

"Baby names." Shay offered him a soft smile. "We have to call our baby something other than Baby Brownstone."

James grunted. "Sure. I know what I want if it's a boy."

"James Junior?"

He shook his head. "Thomas James Brownstone."

Shay's gaze dipped to the dog and then back up to her husband. "If we name our son Thomas, he'll technically have the same name as the family dog. Are you okay with that?"

"I don't give a shit. The dog's named after the closest thing I had to a father in this life, a servant of the Church who gave his life to help protect me. I've got no problem naming my dog after Father Thomas, or my son, or anything else. Shit, for that matter, Thomas is a great dog. And if anyone starts trouble with our son Thomas, he'll finish it. That's the Brownstone way."

"I eagerly await calls from kindergarten. 'Excuse me, Mrs. Brownstone, your son took down half the playground today while shouting, 'Don't disrespect my dad's priest!' That's before they start going off about how we need to have a discussion about proper restraint."

"Don't start shit if you don't want shit. Simple." James shrugged.

Shay smirked. "He's not even born yet. Let's dial it down. Fine, I get how important Father Thomas was to you, so I don't have a problem with the name, and it's not like I have some perfect name in mind."

James' shoulders and neck relaxed. He hadn't even realized they'd tensed up so much. He'd expected Shay to push back more on the name.

"One thing, though." Shay narrowed her eyes. "If you get a middle name, I want a middle name."

"If it's a girl, sure. Why not?"

"Got any first-name preferences?"

James rubbed his chin and furrowed his brow. "How about Mary?"

"You're so Catholic. Naming her Mary's not going to guarantee anything, you know." Shay winked. "They both sound good. Mary Shay Brownstone or Thomas James Brownstone. We in agreement?"

"Yeah." James smiled. "We are. I thought you were going to suggest something crazy."

Shay arched an eyebrow. "Crazy?"

"Some archaeology shit. Like 'Hatshepsut.'"

Shay laughed. "Since when do you pay attention to pharaohs from ancient Egypt?" She eyed him. "Did someone tell you the Egyptians had a secret barbeque recipe?"

*Shit, how did she guess so easily?*

James averted his eyes. "Maybe."

Shay sighed contentedly. "I love you, James, but I sometimes wonder if you would have sold out the planet if the Vax had shown up with a book of sauce recipes."

James grinned. "Nah. Whispy could have just absorbed it from the other symbionts."

"Always thinking, huh? Since we're discussing baby names, we should talk about if we're going to find out the gender of the baby. I've still got several weeks before they can do that, maybe more than a month, but it doesn't hurt to talk about it now."

"What do you think?" James asked.

"I think…" Shay furrowed her brow and licked her lips. "I've never been much for surprises, but that's because surprises used to mean I might end up dead, but it's been a long time since that was a real concern, and this is a nothing but a good thing. It might be fun to not know."

"People might get pissy if we don't find out."

Shay scoffed. "Yeah, like either you or I give two shits what other people think. You know how I feel. The question is, how do *you* feel about all of it?"

James stared at his feet for a moment as he considered the possibilities, then looked up and nodded. "Fuck it. Let's wait. You're right. It'll be fun."

Shay grinned. "Yeah. It *is* fun, isn't it? Now that Alison's little dark wizard problem has been taken care of, this is the perfect time to add someone new to this family. I just need to take it easy. It doesn't hurt if I don't do a tomb raid for a while. It's not like we need the money or the artifacts." Her smile faltered, and she pointed at him. "You got your exercise with the dark wizards, but you need to get back to what you were originally planning."

"Huh? I'm at the restaurant all the time. What are you talking about?"

Shay shook her head and gestured back and forth. "The pacing, remember? Sure, we just had a nice conversation and you're calm now, but I know you're still worried about the kid deep down. Before Alison called you, you were planning a road trip, and I think you should take one so you can have some time to process things without me in your face or having to deal with the day-to-day concerns of running the restaurant. I know you barely pay attention to the agency, so that's always a fun time for you when you do decide to do something, but I don't think ass-kicking will relax you this time."

James frowned. "I'm handling shit all right."

"I'm not saying you aren't." Shay let out a long sigh. "We've been married for a while now, and all that time, you've been great about being open with me, but that's because we haven't had anything like this happen. A level five showing up? Big deal. That's just another notch for the Brownstone Victory belt, but a baby? That's actually new. So I think you should go on a road trip. When you're not pacing, you're staring into the mirror and muttering about kids."

"That's not muttering, it's thinking out loud." James' hands twitched, and he resisted the urge to rise and pace. "Okay. I do kind of want to take a road trip, but I was thinking of waiting until the summer."

Shay stared at him, her face contorted in pained disbelief. "The *summer?*"

James shrugged. "That's when the best barbeque events happen."

"There's no way in hell I want you puttering around and eating sauced meat anywhere near the time I'm ready to pop." Shay shook a finger. "That's not a good idea, and you'll just pace for months and mutter if you wait that long. You need time to process things now, and I'm telling you, as your wife and a woman who just loves you—go ahead, take some time away from home, enjoy all the brisket and let the news finally and totally sink in. No, I'm not telling you, I'm practically *begging* you, damn it."

James scratched his ear. "Nadina is opening up a new place in Denver next week. She invited me. I could go there."

While James couldn't claim he was close friends with the Light Elf pitmaster, they had spent time together at several barbeque events in the last few years, and most people would at least consider them friendly acquaintances. She'd invited him to her openings before and he'd turned her down, worried about the crowds and annoying media.

Nadina thrived under attention. It was probably why she had so many restaurants. She'd come a long way since being a contestant on *Barbeque Wars* and having people question if an elf should even be cooking barbeque.

Shay bobbed her head, relief spreading across her face. "Going to Denver sounds like a good plan. Go. Have fun doing barbeque shit. Hit a bunch of great places along the way, and think about all the barbeque you can shove into our kid in the future."

James grinned. "Okay, I'll do it."

"I assume you'll be stopping off at Jesse Rae's along the way?"

"What would a barbeque road trip be without it?" James resisted the urge to snort. It wasn't as if Shay was trying to challenge his love of Jesse Rae's.

Shay smiled. "Then you should visit Trey and Zoe. You haven't seen either of them in a few months, and phone calls and messages aren't the same thing."

"They've got their own shit to worry about, but yeah, I'll do that."

Given the way Trey had been running things in Vegas, he could have easily broken away from the Brownstone Agency and started his own bounty hunting agency, but he'd made it clear he had no intention of doing that.

Shay's smile turned evil. "And since you're not leaving until next week, we can still go to our thing tomorrow."

James groaned. "I've got nothing against having dinner with Tyler and Maria, but does it have to be at some fancy-ass place?"

"Yes. Yes, it does." Shay winked. "So clench and get ready. You can stand a little bit of pain before all your barbeque pleasure. And let me be the one to break the news to them."

# CHAPTER TWO

James had never gotten comfortable with the concept of a restaurant with a dress code. He wasn't going to complain about Shay's low-cut, high-slit scarlet dress, but even the glorious sight was almost too high a price to pay for the tie and jacket he was forced to wear. This was the uniform they'd make him wear in Hell.

Even though Shay mercifully limited trips to upscale restaurants to about once a quarter, it never made the eventual donning of a choking tie any more comfortable, or the dread over the food choice any less. Usually, he could get by with a steak, but the seafood joint chosen for tonight's dining lacked even that safe option.

The restaurant's menu boasted about their fresh seafood, but James would have given a diamond for a juicy steak. Shay had tricked him. He had assumed they would at least offer surf and turf.

*What's a meal without at least a little beef or pork? Sauce optional.*

While James didn't hate fish, at least cooked fish, he'd

never been overly fond of it, either. Even the baked halibut on his fork lacked the satisfaction of a half-assed-executed steak, let alone the brilliant intricacies of God's second-greatest gift to man: barbeque.

*Maybe if I ate a fish with legs, it'd taste better. Shit. Doesn't that basically mean eating frogs? Fuck that.*

The restaurant's dim lighting was supposed to be atmospheric, but it mostly made it hard to see. That, along with the wide spacing of the tables, provided a slight advantage by isolating James, Shay, Tyler, and Maria. From what Shay had said, Tyler had picked the place, and he'd had to pull a few strings to get a reservation since the restaurant only served dinner and a small number of diners.

Reservations were another thing that annoyed James. Scheduling an order for pickup was one thing, but turning a place into some sort of contest for entry went against his belief that great food should be shared, even if he had a very different definition of what great food was than the chef at the seafood place.

*Just have to put in my time, and then I'll be safe for a few months.*

Tyler and Maria sat across the table, the former looking far too comfortable in his black suit. Maria was wearing a flattering black dress. Shay, Tyler, and Maria had been discussing other restaurants they might want to hit in the future. The latter two had become the Brownstones' official couple partners for fancy dining.

All the choices sounded terrible, but some were bound to have at least a few different steak options. Judging by the look on Tyler's face as he smiled down at his own plate, he didn't share James' opinion of the current food.

"I was just thinking that it's been a while since we've all gotten together." Tyler swirled the wine in his glass, an easy smile on his face. He took a sip. "This was a good choice. I'm glad I picked it. It's always nice to find a new place to take clients to when I'm schmoozing, and you never know if a place is going to live up to its reputation."

*Shit. I* wish *it wasn't living up to its reputation.*

"Everything still going okay?" Shay lowered her fork. "You were having trouble with that attempted industrialist kidnapping case last time I heard."

Tyler shook his head. "Everything's fine. I got that entire thing taken care of." He snickered. "You know, a few years back when I decided to shift over to the security investigation business, I thought I was making a mistake. I kept telling myself, 'Those rich assholes will be more trouble than they're worth. Stay in your lane, Tyler.' But now I'm making more money than I know what to do with, and I don't have to spend as much time around scum. It's refreshing." He surveyed the room and nodded as if satisfied that none of the aforementioned scum was present to hear his complaints. "And we're finally living the lifestyle Maria and I deserve."

His wife rolled her eyes. "I told you from the beginning you should do something like that. You were just too obsessed with being King of the Dirtbags. I never understood the appeal of that garbage, but I'm an ex-cop, so of course, I wouldn't."

Tyler smirked. "You married me. Does that mean you were Queen of the Dirtbags for a while?"

"Yes, it does." Maria lifted her chin haughtily. "Queen Maria the First of the Kingdom of the Dirtbags is not amused."

James picked up his water and took a sip. He'd wanted a beer, but he didn't recognize any of the brands. That might imply he had an unrefined palate when it came to beer, but he didn't care. It was hard to go wrong with water.

Shay took a deep breath. "This wasn't just me wanting to get James out of the house and into a nice suit. We've got news we wanted to share."

Tyler's gaze flicked between Shay and James. "News? Why does that sound scary?" His face twitched.

Shay laughed. "It's nothing bad. It's just…I'm pregnant."

Maria's eyes widened, and she gasped. "Wow. Seriously?"

Shay nodded. "Delivery should be around the middle of July."

"Congrats, Shay."

"Yeah, uh, congrats," Tyler mumbled as he stared at James. "Uh, not to be a dick…" he continued, his voice low.

Maria scoffed. "Does that sentence ever end in a good way? 'Not to be a dick, but you're the best person I've ever met!'"

James locked eyes with Tyler. He knew what was coming. Maria and Tyler had learned the truth about his alien heritage a couple of years prior. James had wondered if the former info broker would use it against him, but Tyler's only response had been to say, "So much shit about you makes sense now, Brownstone, and I don't feel as bad about losing out to Superman."

"I'm just saying…" Tyler licked his lips. "I thought that

wasn't, you know, possible. It's not like you two don't have a healthy sex life."

James grunted.

Shay smirked.

Maria shook her head and sighed. "For a guy who is always riding James for his lack of tact, you sure are being pretty embarrassing right now."

Tyler shrugged. "It's a legitimate observation."

The group fell silent as the waiter came to check on them.

Once the waiter had retreated several yards, Tyler leaned back toward James. "I'm just saying you're not exactly newlyweds, and you haven't had a kid yet. It's been years."

"Shit changed," James replied with a shrug. "Whispy changed me."

Maria reached over to pat Shay's hand. "That's great." She ran a hand through her graying hair. "I'm a little jealous. I got married too late to King Dirtbag over there, and I don't have any nieces or nephews, but now I'll have the chance to be the most awesome godmother in the world to make up for it."

Tyler stared down at his half-eaten lobster, his face pinched. "I'm having trouble processing this. How does it even work?"

Maria pulled her hand back. "Do I need to explain it to you? When a Mommy Brownstone and a Daddy Brownstone love each other very much, sometimes they get together at night and have fun. Then, nine months later, a baby is born."

"Very funny." Tyler grimaced. "Come on, am I the only

one who's having trouble thinking of James with a kid? The Granite Ghost is spawning? This is breaking my brain a little."

Maria narrowed her eyes. "He already has a kid. A very successful kid."

"But she came with miles on her already."

James shrugged. He didn't really care what Tyler thought, even if the man had hit a few points he'd been thinking about too. It wasn't crazy for someone to think the idea of him with a young kid at least a little odd.

"'The Granite Ghost is spawning?'" Shay let out a low laugh. "As opposed to me? I'm not exactly a woman whose life screams 'maternal.'"

Tyler waved his hand and looked around the room as if shocked that not everyone was in an uproar about the news, even if they hadn't heard it. "I can see it now: your kid wandering around the preschool breaking little bullies' heads and calling them stupid dumb asses. The Brownstone School Effect."

"Preschool?" Shay grinned at James. "We were thinking of kindergarten, but preschool could work, too."

"All Brownstones do what they need to do," rumbled James. "Regardless of age. Alison was kicking ass when she needed to as a teenager."

Tyler pointed at him. "See, this is what I'm talking about." He laughed. "Most *normal people* would be like, 'No, of course, my kid isn't going to run around taking down everyone who threatens him.'"

Maria elbowed him. "Don't be annoying."

Tyler gave her a pained look. "Not being annoying. Just being real."

"I don't care." James grunted. "I'm not normal. *We're* not normal. But the whole thing is kind of different. Since I'm mostly retired from bounty hunting, it makes me worry less about family stuff. I can be there for the kid without too much trouble. Cleaning up the trash once or twice a year won't be a problem, even if Shay needs extra help."

Shay nodded. "See? Not a big deal. Alison knows already, but you two are the first people otherwise to be told."

Maria smiled. "I'm honored."

Tyler grinned.

Shay smirked. "If you want to sell the information, you better hurry before we start telling everyone."

"I wasn't going to sell it." Tyler looked insulted.

"You were thinking about it."

Tyler shrugged. "It's not like I'm totally out of the old game, you know. Instincts and all that."

"I don't care," James replied. "It's not gonna be a big secret."

*Why? I could have told Mack, but Shay's right, and so is Tyler. I'm still trying to process this shit. The more people I tell, the more I have to face it.*

A thoughtful look passed over Maria's face. "Retirement, huh?"

The other three all looked at her.

"What about it?" Shay asked. "It's been a while for James."

"It wasn't his retirement I was thinking about." Maria's gaze grew distant, almost wistful. "I was a cop for a long time, and I've been a bounty hunter for a long time too, almost thirty years altogether. I've been kicking scumbag asses for decades. James left this bounty-hunting game, and you…" she looked around, "…you focused on academics over your *old* career. Tyler switched too, but I keep thinking lately, 'What would it be like if I retired and got away from a job that requires me risking getting shot at or fireballed?' That might not be such a bad thing."

Tyler blinked. "You never mentioned this to me. Not that I'm complaining. I've always thought your job was too dangerous. I mean, you work for the Brownstone Agency." He nodded at James. "He doesn't work for his own agency."

James shrugged. "Not because it's dangerous."

"Well, yeah. Nothing's too dangerous for you."

James grinned. "Besides, I beat down enough pieces of shit to last me a hundred years. I've earned a little barbeque time."

"I feel the same way," Maria admitted. "Not the barbeque thing, just something else." She sighed. "I've been thinking about it for a while. Shay being pregnant just really brought it home." She offered Shay an apologetic smile. "Sorry. I didn't mean to hijack your announcement."

Shay shook her head. "I've got months and months to be the center of attention. If you want to talk about retirement, might as well do it with your friends, right? We've both done the big switch to a radically different career."

Maria took a deep breath. She picked up her wine glass and downed a large gulp. "Working for the agency pays well, but it's not like I need the money. I haven't for a long time."

"I know the feeling, and unless you've been lying to me all these years, the job was never about excitement."

Maria shook her head. "I never was a danger junkie. I

always hated those guys when I was on the force. They're the kind of cops who get other cops killed. My best days on the force were those when nothing happened." She turned to James. "You adjusted pretty easily."

James swallowed his latest bite of halibut—still not as good as steak, no matter how many bites he took. "Just worked out that way. Retirement's pretty cool. Simpler in some ways, more complicated in others. I kick a few asses a year just to remind people of who I am, but I focus on the barbeque." He set his fork down. "I don't know. Maybe I was always supposed to be focusing on the barbeque, and the bounty hunting was always a distraction. Mysterious ways, and all that."

Shay winked. "You just needed the love of a good woman and a daughter."

James shrugged. "Probably."

Shay grinned. "I also don't know if it's true we're technically retired. We just switched jobs. Same thing with Tyler."

"It's close enough," Maria replied. "You switched to something less dangerous. Call it a midlife crisis. I'd like to go to work in the morning and not worry about getting blown up."

Tyler nodded quickly. "I'm pro the not-getting-blown-up plan. It's like you said—you don't need the money. *We* don't need the money. I know you like being a leader at the agency, but you've told me tons of times about how you've built a good team."

Maria sighed. "I know, I know. That's not the thing holding me back."

"What is, then?" Shay asked.

"I don't know what I'd do. I don't have some big passion like barbeque."

"You could work with me," Tyler suggested.

Maria chuckled. "I'm a big believer in 'absence makes the heart grow fonder.' We've both got too big of personalities to work together."

"Oh." Tyler looked crestfallen.

"Why do you have to do anything?" James asked.

"Because I'm not the kind of woman who can just sit around all day doing nothing," Maria replied. "I wasn't lying when I said I've never been a danger junkie, but I want to feel like I'm accomplishing, something, anything, with my day. I don't know. Shay's got her academic career and a kid, and it's making me think."

"You could get a pet," Shay offered.

A grin grew on Maria's face. "Or twelve."

Tyler groaned. "Ugh. At least kids grow up into adults you can have a decent conversation with."

Maria shook her head. "Enough about me. I've got plenty of time to think. We should toast." She raised her glass. "To the future Brownstone, the terror of his preschool."

Shay and Tyler laughed and raised their glasses.

James grunted as he lifted his. Discomfiting thoughts crawled into the back of his mind. He wouldn't call them doubts, or not true ones, anyway. Years of marriage with Shay had left him confident they could face any challenge.

*Will I be a good dad? Who knows? It'll be hard to fuck up too much when I've got a good wife and friends around.*

*But why do I feel this tight knot in my stomach like something's gonna fuck up my happiness?*

James frowned down at his halibut. He wouldn't be feeling this strongly if he had a decent brisket in front of him.

*Is this just me needing to get some shit out of my system?*

The conversation blurred into the background as Shay explained their name choices and the desire to be surprised by the baby's gender.

Maria wasn't the only one who needed to figure a few things out.

CHAPTER THREE

James stepped out of the kitchen into the front of his small barbeque restaurant, the Pig and Cow. The dining room was modest, filled with eight simple white wooden tables with chairs. There was no tv on the wall, which was instead covered with pictures and plaques from competitions. A modest assortment of trophies resting on shelves completed the decorations.

It might take James a while to catch up with Jesse Rae's, but he was on his way. He'd come damned close to beating them during their last head-to-head showdown.

*Maybe I'll never reach the level of Jesse Rae's, but targeting the best of the best means I'll get better. No point in beating some pitmaster with weak-ass barbeque and sauce that tastes like salty water.*

A weary-looking man in a rumpled suit stood near the front counter, his hand held out to accept a large plastic bag filled with several smaller bags of ribs, their scent drifting from the counter.

Most of James' customers were like the man: they

ordered ahead for pickup. Enjoying good barbeque was about the taste, not irrelevant ambiance like the upscale seafood place. Having a smaller building also made it easier to control crowds.

That issue hadn't been as pronounced in recent years, with most people understanding a customer came to the Pig and Cow for good food, not for James Brownstone. On occasion, though, a news story would remind non-regulars about who was running the restaurant and cause a surge of inconveniently annoying interest.

Renee, the employee handling the transaction with the weary customer, gave James a polite nod before returning her attention to the other man. "Thank you for your business, sir. Please come again."

The tables were filled with regulars, including Luis and his friends. The man was there almost every night, and had been since the place opened. The regulars all nodded at James before returning to their conversations, beer, and food.

The suited man lowered the bag, his eyes widening when he saw James. "I've ordered pickup like a half-dozen times, and I've never actually seen you. I wasn't even sure if you worked here anymore."

*You could have just asked.*

James grunted. "I'm not always here, and when I am, I mostly stay in the kitchen. I own a barbeque restaurant to cook barbeque, and it's hard to do that if I'm up front chatting with customers." He shrugged.

The man nodded. "Of course, of course. Could I get your autograph? Maybe a picture? I'll pay whatever you want. Please. I've read all about you."

"I'm not gonna make you pay for a picture. That's stupid." James snorted and reached under the counter to pull out a menu. He held out his hand to Renee.

She smiled, pulled a pen out of her apron pocket, and gave it to him.

James scribbled his autograph on the menu along with the note, *Barbeque is life* before handing it to the suited man. "I better not find that shit on some auction site." He narrowed his eyes. "Understood?"

The suited man shook his head and reached into his pocket for his phone. "No, no. Never." He lifted his phone with a smile on his face. "Say cheese."

James stared at the man, not smiling but not frowning either. It was his standard expression for fans.

The customer put his phone back in his pocket and took a few deep breaths, staring down at the menu before picking up his bag. "Thank you, Mr. Brownstone." He practically skipped out of the restaurant, his bag swinging.

"That was almost as annoying as the guy who lives in Alison's condo," James muttered.

Luis laughed from his table. "There are worse things in the world than being famous. Most people want others to recognize them for something. People recognize you for a lot of things, but you complain. Don't you want people to enjoy the restaurant and your food?"

The front door opened and Mack stepped in, whistling.

"Yeah, I want people to enjoy this place," James continued, "but because they like my food, not because of a bounty I took down or a story they read about me on the internet or Chile or whatever bullshit they're talking about on any given day."

27

Mack grinned. "You complaining about people liking you again, James? You want everyone to hate you?" The retired cop-turned-pitmaster ran a hand over his coarse gray hair. The years hadn't put too many wrinkles in his dark skin, but they had been far less kind to the covering up top. Mack never complained.

*He never talks about how I look like I've stopped aging. I wasn't as old as Mack to begin with, but I'm in my forties now. Of course, I've always been an ugly sonofabitch, so maybe that's helping people not realize what's going on.*

James shrugged. "I don't think I'll ever get comfortable with this celebrity shit. My brain isn't built for it. Shay says the same kind of thing whenever I complain, or tells me I can go hide in the mountains if I think it's too much."

Several people in the dining room chuckled. They'd all heard the complaints numerous times. They'd also all gotten their pictures and autographs a long time ago. Even if they'd come for the man, they had stayed for the food, and that was fine with James.

Luis gestured to James and shook his head. "Get a load of James here, living in LA and being all shy and not wanting attention. Talk to half the waiters and waitresses in town, and they're all like, 'Oh, I'm just doing this as a side gig until my big role comes through or King Oriceran decides he needs a bunch of human actors.' If I was you, I'd be like, 'I'm James Brownstone. You want a picture with me, you better give me a gold bar and your first-born child. Because that's how good I am, man.'"

His tablemates snickered.

James frowned, his gaze flicking to Mack. The coming

explanation wouldn't do much to weaken his celebrity image.

*Shit. Every time I think things will go away, they don't. I thought the adoption hearing made things get too big, and then the Council brought more attention, but at least with the Battle of LA, most people didn't understand what was going on or that I was involved.*

James grimaced. He really would have to flee to the mountains if the general public ever found out he had fought off an alien invasion, including a second wave meant to end all life on Earth. The attention would be endless.

"Uh, Mack?" James began. "I should tell you now I'm taking a few days off, maybe a week. Not until next week, but that's not a huge amount of notice. Sorry."

Mack stepped behind the counter, his relaxed smile remaining. "Going on vacation? I can't say that I'm surprised. I kind of wondered after some of the other recent stuff."

"Yeah, just a little road trip," James explained. "Nadina invited me to the opening of her new place in Denver. I keep turning her down, but I'll take her up on it this time."

An excited murmur swept the room, and several people looked his way with eager expressions.

"Nadina?" Luis' growing smile almost ate his face. "There's just something about a woman that hot. And she's got magic, too. Damn. Complete package."

Renee rolled her eyes and disappeared into the back.

James shrugged. "Who cares what she looks like or that she can do magic? What do those have to do with barbeque? She doesn't use spells on anything she cooks, and she can't be at all her restaurants at once anyway even if she did."

Luis groaned and shook his head. He eyed James with a mixture of pity and disgust. "That's the problem with you married dudes. You don't see any woman other than yours. I'm telling you, she's hot. Not like, just hot because she's an elf, but hot-hot, you know? That's all I'm saying. This isn't rocket science, James."

His tablemates bobbed their heads quickly, their faces communicating their sincerity and disappointment in James' reaction.

Mack chuckled quietly. "I'm sure being attractive didn't hurt her career, but I've tasted her barbeque. It's the real thing. Do I always personally enjoy all of her flavor combinations? Nope, but that's the thing about this kind of food: everyone has their preferences, and anyone who can bring some freshness without going too far is fine by me." He grabbed a dark-blue apron from under the counter and slipped it over his head.

"Her barbeque could be the worst thing in the world as long as she keeps looking like that, and she's an elf, so it'll be a long time before she stops looking hot." Luis smirked at James and speared a piece of his brisket with a fork. "You're lucky you're so damned good at grilling, James. With a face like yours, you have to have skill, even if you *are* famous. Fame doesn't keep people coming back for food. No offense."

"None taken," James rumbled. "I stopped caring about how I looked a long time ago, but I'll never stop caring about how good my barbeque tastes."

A few people finished their meals. They stood and filed out, smiling at James and Mack as they left.

Mack nodded to the departing customers. "Why the sudden vacation? Is it a true vacation, or is it another thing like that Canada trip?" He held up a hand. "If you can't tell me, that's fine. I know the government pokes you every once in a while to beg for help."

James grunted. "Nothing like that," he rumbled. "Canada's done and over, and it's nothing more than I said—a road trip to check out Nadina's new place."

Everyone left in the room was familiar enough with James' disdain for non-automobile transportation to not bother questioning why he was driving to Colorado instead of flying, or even, given his resources, using a portal.

Luis' smile finally disappeared for the first time in the conversation. "Canada, huh? I wasn't going to ask because I know that kind of shit pisses you off, but the news was saying there was some like crazy stuff up there. That you and your daughter and her friends all upped and saved Vancouver from some serious-ass monsters."

James shook his head. "It wasn't about saving Vancouver. It was about taking down a bunch of assholes who couldn't take a hint. Those same assholes thought they had a doomsday artifact we couldn't counter, but they were wrong. It was personal."

Luis' smile returned, and he cackled. "The latest recipients of the Harriken Award for Long-term Stupidity." He picked up a rib. "Some people don't learn until it's too late."

"Exactly." James allowed himself a tight smile. He might not be as merciful as Alison, but he didn't go out of his way to destroy organizations if they left him well enough alone, particularly in the last few years of his semi-retirement. He took a deep breath. "This is all because of Shay. She suggested I take the road trip. She thinks it'll give me time to think about some stuff that's come up."

Mack gave him a look of a concern, his gaze flicking to Luis and some of the other customers before coming back to James. "Is everything all right?" he asked, his voice low.

"It's fine." James stared at the wall. "I just found out Shay's pregnant. I'm going to be a dad."

Luis hopped up from the table, pumping his fist in the air and cheering. The other customers joined him or clapped. Mack smiled.

A warmth passed through James.

"Congrats, James," Luis shouted. "I didn't even know you were trying, or have been trying and it fina…" He shut up with a glare from Mack. "Sorry, sorry. Yeah, privacy and all that. Wow. Congrats. Another Brownstone in LA. All the schools are going to get cleaned up now. Brownstone Effect all around."

James shook his hand and chuckled. "Maybe, but a kid's still a kid."

"Your daughter was doing bounties when she was a teenager." Luis lifted his hands and his face twisted into an incredulous expression. "You might have mostly hung up the cape, Superman, but she's all the news all the time, which means your new kid is going to end up on the news all the time. I'm telling you, in ten years, it'll be like, 'Every gang in LA surrenders because Little Brownstone has declared war on crime after they stole his bike.'" He rubbed his hands together. "Oh, man, if it's a boy, will you call it Luis? Man, I would be so honored. Come on, man. Please?"

"No," James declared flatly. "We've got names already."

Luis slapped his thigh. "Damn. It was worth a try. You can't blame me."

Mack stood behind the sales terminal and tapped in a few commands. "So you hear about your kid, and you decide to go on a road trip?"

*Shit. I didn't think about what this sounds like.*

James cleared his throat. "I was thinking about making a road trip in the summer, but Shay doesn't want me gone around her due date, and she really thinks it's a good idea."

"Wise." Mack nodded. "You never know how these things will turn out. Babies come when they want to come, and once that kid is born, you need to be there to help your woman out." He extended his hand. "Congratulations, James. I'm sure you'll be as great a father as you are a bounty hunter and pitmaster."

James shook his hand. "All I can do is my best."

Luis raised a glass of Coke. "To Little Brownstone."

Everyone raised a glass. "To Little Brownstone!"

# CHAPTER FOUR

James inhaled deeply, the delicious scents of cayenne and vinegar wafting up from the ribs on the grill and filling his nostrils.

Bliss. Perfection. Man couldn't have heaven on Earth, but he could get damned close with enough spices and good grilling technique.

It didn't matter how many times James smelled it; the scent never lost its power. Some might call it an obsession, but he didn't mind. It'd been years since he'd switched his focus from ass-kicking to barbeque, and he'd never regretted the decision. Ass-kicking had become the distraction. Perhaps it always had been.

*How would my life had been different if I'd gone into barbeque from the beginning?*

James would never claim running a barbeque restaurant matched the importance of dealing with threats like the Council or the Vax, but he had put in his time, and he still occasionally took down a bad guy or two. His focus on family, friends, and his community filled him with a satisfaction he'd never thought possible when he was living alone with Leeroy. Before Alison. Before Shay.

*The years have flown by. Remembering everything so well is kind of annoying at times. I wonder if I could have let go better if I didn't have this kind of memory?*

A few years back, James finally had the thought to ask Whispy if his memory was something all Vax possessed. To his surprise, he learned that not only did all Vax *not* have such perfect memories, but that it had not been Whispy's intent to give James that sort of ability. It had been a side-effect of some of the other modifications the symbiont had performed shortly after his arrival on Earth.

*Where do I end and Whispy begins? I don't even wear him all that often anymore, but he's modified me so much. I'm not even the same species I was born as. I'm an alien who can have a kid with a human.*

James snorted and shook his head. It didn't help to get lost in possibilities. The symbiont did what James required when he needed it, and didn't seem to mind sitting around on standby most of the year, even if he sometimes seemed frustrated or almost sad that no other Vax had shown up in the last eight years. Whispy didn't really seem to perceive the passage of time.

Fortunately, the Vax, unlike the Harriken, had gotten the message in one battle. They were off ravaging half the galaxy for all James knew, but they hadn't dared showed up again on Earth or Oriceran, and that was fine with him. He wasn't a superhero; it wasn't his duty to protect the galaxy. He would stick to running his restaurant and taking care of his family, including the child coming in the summer.

*Life's complicated in its own way, but it's not as complicated as it could be. No aliens other than me to worry about. The Alliance hasn't so much as sniffed my way since LA, and from what Johnston keeps saying, they never will.*

A harsh shout from the dining room ripped James from his introspection. With a frown, he looked toward the kitchen door. Some of the regulars like Luis could get a little loud, but they never yelled, and for that matter, Luis and his buddies had left an hour ago. Maybe someone just really liked their brisket.

The door squeaked open and Renee poked her head through, her brown eyes filled with concern. "James, I think you better get out here. Mack still isn't back from his errand, and there's…trouble I need your help with."

James narrowed his eyes. "Trouble? What sort of trouble?"

Renee sighed. "It'd be easier if you just came out and saw."

"Absolute shit!" a deep male voice shouted from the dining room. "I don't know how people can't say this isn't absolute shit. I dare you to tell me it's not, you stupid brainwashed assholes."

*What the hell?*

James checked the temperature gauge one last time before lowering the grill's lid and marching toward the door. This didn't sound like a minor customer service complaint.

There were times that being the Granite Ghost in addition to being a pitmaster was helpful. Every once in a while, some idiot drank a few too many beers, but even drunk idiots didn't have the balls to stand up to James

37

Brownstone. Not calling the cops was a point of pride for the Pig and Cow. The police had better things to do than handle drunken fools at a restaurant, and there was pretty much nothing on Earth James couldn't handle.

The heavy weight of his amulet rested against his chest, the metal spacer keeping his chest from touching it. He doubted he'd need that level of help, but it was good to have Whispy there in case the angry customer turned out to be some strange Oriceran assassin.

James emerged from the door to find a broad-shouldered man in jeans and a greasy t-shirt reading Kiss My Ass seated at a table, a tray of ribs in front of him and a scowl all but carved into his face.

The angry man's head jerked toward James, and he stood and glared. "You cook this shit? I will understand if you're embarrassed to admit it."

"I'm not embarrassed by anything I've ever cooked." James' face tightened. "And yeah, I did. You got a problem with your ribs? They look fine to me."

"Looks aren't everything. Taste is, so yeah, I got a problem with my ribs." The man leaned over to pick up a rib and dropped back to the tray, his face pinched in disgust. "I have a big problem with the fact that these are the worst fucking ribs I've ever tasted in my life. They wouldn't inflict this kind of shit on guys in prison."

A few of the other customers glared at the man, including Gertrude, one of James' regulars. The old woman was pushing eighty and credited beer and barbeque for her longevity. Her hand rested atop her cane as she tried to burn through the man with a baleful look. Some of the younger men at other tables looked just as displeased.

"It's a free country, and you're free to be a complete dumbass." James pointed to the door. "There's the exit. You don't like the food? That's fine. Nothing's keeping you here. Don't let the door hit you on the way out."

The man shook his head. "Fuck that. You owe me. I want my money back for having to suffer through that so-called meal."

"No refunds," James growled. "Now get out of here before you really piss me off."

"No way." The man slammed his hand on the table. The tray, plates, and silverware rattled. "I came here because of how good this place is supposed to be, but it's literally the worst barbeque I've ever had in my life. I drove all the way here from Santa Monica, and now I'm going to have to stop somewhere else because of this shit you're peddling as barbeque. I wouldn't be surprised if I end up in the ER with food poisoning."

James took a deep breath. He doubted the cops would appreciate him kicking a non-bounty through a window just because the man was talking shit about his barbeque, but the rude customer was pushing him to his limit. He had to admire the man's bravery as much as his stupidity.

*This is the problem with customer-fucking-service.*

"Leave." James folded his arms over his chest. "Leave now before you piss me off."

The man sneered. "I'm not leaving without my money back. Maybe I should stand outside and tell everyone who is coming into this place how shitty this barbeque is. You like that? I got nothing better to do before I get the shits from your horrible barbeque."

James stepped out from behind the counter. The angry

customer smirked as the pitmaster approached his table, rumbling low in his chest.

With a quick snatch, James grabbed one of the ribs and took a bite. He chewed slowly, letting the various notes of flavor play over his tongue before swallowing.

"Are you high?" James asked. "Because you have to be high if you think that tastes bad. Or maybe you're just drunk?"

"I'm not high," the man shouted, throwing his hands up. He pointed to a glass of water. "And I haven't been drinking. I have a right to my opinion, and in my opinion, your barbeque is crap."

James tossed the rib back on the table. "There's nothing wrong with that rib, but you're acting like it was the worst thing you've ever eaten. The only explanation I can think of is you're high, or you're just a dumbass who has never had barbeque before. Some elf keep you locked up on Oriceran for five hundred years, and you're just getting to Earth now?"

"I've had the best barbeque out there." The man scoffed. "Just because you're coasting on fame doesn't mean I'm wrong. Everyone knows if you weren't James Brownstone, this place would have folded within a couple of months. I'm just the only one brave enough to say it."

*Yeah, you're brave. I'll give you that, and only that.*

"Shame on you," shouted Gertrude from her table, her face red. "You're a terrible person. Get out of here."

Several other customers nodded their agreement, their faces contorted in anger.

"Quiet, old woman. This isn't your business." The angry

customer turned back toward James, his lips curled into a sneer. "I might as well eat shit if I'm going to have to eat that stuff. It's basically the same."

Gertrude stood shakily and shook her head. "Absolutely no manners."

"This is still my restaurant," James muttered, his jaw clenched. "And I'm telling you to get the hell out. We reserve the right to serve who we want, and I'm now telling you to get out."

"Or what?" the man shouted. "You're not going to call the cops." He stomped forward until he stood right in front of James, his fetid breath infiltrating James' nostrils. "You're James Brownstone. You're not going to do something weak like that. If you want me gone, you'll need to throw me out yourself. I dare you to do it. I bet you don't have the balls to do it."

Several other customers shook their heads, disbelief on their faces. Gertrude left her table and, using her cane, started making her way toward James and the angry customer.

*Now he's scaring off customers. Fuck it. I guess I don't have any choice.*

James locked eyes with the angry customer. "You really, really don't want to make me pissed, asshole."

"Or what? I'm no criminal. I've got no bounty." The man stepped back and slapped his chest. "I'm just a man who happens to think you can't cook barbeque. That's not a crime."

"Trespassing is."

"Throw me out then, bitch." The man grinned.

James' nostrils flared. He'd had enough. If he had to deal with trouble with the police, so be it. The asshole in front of him was pushing hard for some pain.

*The only question is, should I throw him through the window or the door? Which would be easiest to fix? Huh. I finally understand how Tyler used to feel.*

Gertrude stopped right behind the man. "Are you going to leave?"

The man kept his attention on James as he shook his head. "No way. I'm not leaving until I get an apology from Brownstone and my money back. I should ask for some extra money for him wasting my time arguing with me."

"Fine." Gertrude whipped her cane up and slammed it into the back of the man's knee with surprising speed.

The man yelped and fell forward when his leg buckled. His stomach slammed into the table. The fall ended with him on the table holding his stomach.

"You bitch," the angry man growled.

James snickered. The rest of the dining room burst out in laughter.

The angry customer sat up and glared at Gertrude. "You're not supposed to hit me."

The old woman lifted her chin, satisfaction and pride in her eyes. "Normally I'd say violence doesn't solve anything, but you're asking for trouble."

"Damn it." The man scrambled to his feet and flung an arm in James' direction. "You're not supposed to hit me. Brownstone is. Damn it. I can't sue some poor-ass old lady on Social Security." He raised a fist. "You just cost me a big settlement, you old bitch."

*Oh, that explains it. He's not brave, he's just greedy.*

The angry man took one step toward the old woman. Several men stood at nearby tables, their eyes narrowed and their fists clenched.

"Stop right there, asshole," James growled. He curled his hand into a fist. "I let you come in here and talk shit about my barbeque even though you were obviously lying. I gave you plenty of chances to leave, and you kept talking crap about my food." He shoved a chair out of the way so hard it crashed into a nearby wall and clattered to the tiled floor, the back cracked. "Now you're pissing off my regulars and threatening an old woman. You want angry Brownstone? You got angry-fucking-Brownstone," he growled.

The other man winced, some of the fire draining from his face.

James gave him a feral grin. "Your brilliant plan was to come in here and piss me off until I punched you? Then you could sue me for a bunch of money?"

The man swallowed, his eyes wide. "Y-you're rich. You could spare some money."

"Are you the dumbest asshole on the planet?" James rumbled. "I thought everyone knew what happened to people who pissed me off. Say you succeeded. Would it be worth getting all your meals through a straw for the rest of your life? Hey, for that matter, you ever been thrown through a window?"

The man grimaced.

The other customers retook their seats, nodding in agreement. Gertrude hobbled her way back over to her table with a satisfied smile on her face.

The now-scared complainer backed toward the exit. "You wouldn't dare. Y-you'd get in trouble."

James scoffed. "You don't know crap about what I might do, especially when people piss me off. I'm a married man now, and I've got a kid on the way. I try to keep it calm, but disrespecting my restaurant as part of some sort of scheme is pretty fucking annoying." He slowly raised his hand and pointed at the door. "People are trying to have a good meal here, and you're ruining the atmosphere. I could beat your ass, but then I'll have to waste time talking to the cops, and I won't be able to cook for any new customers for a few hours because none of my other pitmasters are here. I'm gonna take a page from my daughter and give you one last chance to get the hell out of here instead. Otherwise, we're gonna see how far you can fly after going through my window."

The complainer nodded quickly and sprinted toward the door.

"Wait," James ordered.

The man halted and turned back around, his face pale. He swallowed. "What now?"

"I never forget a face," James explained. "Don't even think about coming here again and trying that bullshit with anyone else. I might be running a restaurant, but I used to be a bounty hunter. Do you really think I can't find and take someone out without the cops finding out?"

The complainer threw open the door. A confused-looking Mack stood on the other side. The other customers cheered.

Mack stared after the fleeing man before entering and closing the door behind him. "Do I even want to know?"

"Just someone who was trying to push me." James walked over to pick up the chair he'd tossed. "Damn. Now I have to replace this, but at least it's cheaper than fixing the window."

Mack glanced at the cracked chair. "It sounds like it's a good time for you to get away."

CHAPTER FIVE

James chuckled as he pushed into Jesse Rae's. Even as he thought about and mentally prepared himself in the days leading up to his trip, he was more satisfied than he expected that the first leg of his journey was complete with his evening arrival in Las Vegas. It was a familiar city with familiar friends and restaurants, and he'd been away for too long.

It was hard for James to ignore the amusing reality that he was getting away from his own barbeque place just to head to another barbeque place.

*It's a barbeque road trip. Maybe the next road trip won't be about barbeque, but the next week is gonna be nothing but sauce and meat for me. No fancy shit.*

James grinned. He loved Shay, but sometimes it was nice to know he could have his favorite food without any risk of having high-end fish shoved at him. It was even worse when he visited Alison since sushi was her favorite food. He'd tried to appreciate it, but its subtleties continued to escape him.

*I don't get it, but it's her mouth and stomach, so I shouldn't complain too much.*

Jesse Rae's hadn't changed much since James had opened his own place, except there were more plaques, trophies, and certificates on the wall. It felt like for every competition the Pig and Cow won, Jesse Rae's won two. The overwhelming number of victories made them start being strategic about which awards they chose to display in their dining room. Victory had created inconvenience.

*A moving target is harder to hit but more satisfying.*

James offered the owner Mike, who stood at the counter, a polite nod before heading toward his destination, a table holding a handsome, dark-skinned young man in an expensive black suit. It was Trey Garfield, the bounty hunter responsible for running the Brownstone Agency satellite office in Las Vegas.

"What's up, big man?" Trey called with a wave. "I know we're always on the phone and whatnot, but it's been too long since I've seen you with these here eyeballs. It's good to see that face of yours. Reminds me that you're real and not just a guy grunting on the phone."

James dropped into a seat. Trays filled with brisket and ribs already covered the table. Trey knew what he liked, and so did Mike, his family, and his employees. Jesse Rae's had catered his wedding, after all, and it wasn't like his taste had changed much in the following years.

James shrugged. "Yeah, I get up my ass about running the restaurant and act like it'll fall apart if I leave, but I've got Mack there. I should visit more often."

"Not blaming you. Don't get me wrong." Trey smiled. "I'm just as guilty. I could visit you when I'm visiting Nana, but I always seem to have an excuse not to lately. Things get busy. You know how things go—responsibility and all that. I guess we both have problems with perspective."

*There's something bothering me about Trey, but what it is? And why is it bothering me all of a sudden?*

"Yeah, responsibility and perspective." James stared at the other man, his eyes narrowing. He'd not paid much attention to the subtle changes in Trey's speech patterns over the last year. The minor diction changes had added up to something major. There was a big and obvious explanation for it, even if Trey had never explicitly suggested it.

*Son of a bitch.*

Trey frowned and looked down at his suit before looking back up at James. "I don't need a bib, big man. I can eat a few ribs without getting my clothes dirty. You've seen me eat barbeque in my suit a million times."

"No. It's not that." James grunted.

"Then what is it?"

James shook his head. "It's just...you don't cuss much anymore. Somehow I knew it without realizing it. Does that make sense?"

"Oh. I see." Trey laughed. "Yeah, I suppose I don't. I thought I'd told you about that, but I don't rightly remember telling you directly." He frowned. "Yeah, told a bunch of people at the agency and Nana and Charlyce, but never you." He shrugged. "It's something that comes with Zoe and me having Little Zoe. It was just a small change at first because I caught her staring at me when I rattled off one of my classic colorful Trey descriptions. I didn't care when she was a baby, but since she's started talking, it's gotten a little uncomfortable."

"And Zoe got mad about it, so you decided to change?"

Trey snorted. "Nope. It's not like my wife cared that I had a gangster's mouth, but it was hard to look at my little girl and not think, 'Oh, man, I can do better by her. Nana tried with me, but I let the streets teach me more than my Nana. Now I have a choice, so I chose to change my habits, and habit became reality. That reality became me." He fluffed his lapels. "It's not like I never do it. I can drop the nice words with the bounties, but it's kind of a contest with myself to keep it clean otherwise. That way I never screw up around Little Zoe. So Smooth Trey came to stay, you know what I'm saying?"

James offered a shallow nod. "Yeah, that makes sense. It's not like I think you *need* to cuss or anything. It's just something I noticed."

"Why is this coming up all of a sudden? I mean, it's been a while now." Trey pointed and grinned. "Oh, I get it. I get it. You're all worried. James Brownstone's gonna have to control his mouth. Being a foul-mouthed bounty hunter-slash-pitmaster won't do when Little Brownstone's toddling along sucking on her thumb."

"Her?" James furrowed his brow. "We don't know the gender yet."

He wasn't sure which he preferred, but he didn't want to set himself up for disappointment by focusing too much on one gender or another. He had a daughter he was proud of, and he wouldn't mind another daughter to be proud of, but he also wouldn't mind a son.

"Fine. His or her thumb." Trey forked a piece of brisket onto his plate. "Don't change anything, though."

"I'll admit the thought had occurred to me. Shit

changes, and people change." James grunted. "Even I can change. I already have."

*Whispy's changed me more than most people know, even the ones I've told the truth about me.*

Trey shook his head as he set his fork down on his plate. "You should have waited to tell me about the kid in person, by the way. The whole 'Oh, let's meet, and oh yeah, I'm gonna have a new kid' thing over the phone was weak, big man.'" He scoffed. "Delivering the news to me like you got a new pair of shoes. Weak! What was that about? You haven't had any trouble?"

"I'm still processing the whole kid thing, but I think I'm okay." James nodded, more for his own benefit than Trey's. "I'm not saying it's not gonna be a big adjustment, but I'm far less...concerned than when Shay first told me. If that makes sense."

"You're okay?" Incredulity crept onto Trey's face. "Seriously?" Somehow, even more suspicion appeared and he clucked his tongue a few times. "Uh-huh. Sure."

James frowned. "Why wouldn't I be? It's a kid, not some CIA rogue squad after me."

"Hey, big man, I knew you before even Shay knew you. I know you gave up on your KISS philosophy, but it's burned into your soul." Trey shook a finger at him. "And I know you're realizing how the kid's gonna make things complicated, and your brain is having trouble handling that even though your heart is happy. No problem admitting that. That's just part of being a new dad. I went through the same thing."

"Sure, maybe I've thought some of that, but how hard can it be?"

Trey stared at James somberly for a few seconds before cackling. "You've got some pretty big delusions, big man, and the Lord's about to shatter them something fierce, but don't worry. I'm here to tell you it's all worth it. Plus, you've got experience at least on the teenage end, and that's the hardest part. Everyone says so. At least when they're little, they still have some respect for you. I wasn't a punk to Nana until I was a teenager."

James took a few bites of a rib, pondering both his child and the flavor for a moment. "How is Nana Garfield? I haven't seen her in a while; going on six months now. Is she doing okay? You know how I am. I don't like asking Charlyce anything personal when she sends me a work message."

Trey scratched his cheek, a thoughtful look settling over him. "I bet you Nana's gonna outlive us all. Yeah, she can't move around like she could, but at least she hasn't caused more trouble for her live-in nurse." He grinned. "At least lately, but she's getting feistier and feistier. By the time she hits a hundred, she might be out of control and fuller of life than ever." He chuckled. "She's earned a few years of that sort of thing, I figure, if only because of all the trouble and heartache I caused her."

James nodded slowly. "If there's anything I can do to help, just let me know. I don't know much about taking care of old people, but I could get stuff for you if you need it."

Trey shook his head. "You did your part years ago when you got the boys and me off the street, and you're still technically paying me even if you don't pay any attention to the agency anymore. Besides, nothing you can do that I can't."

He let out a long, weary sigh. "Nana's as stubborn as she is old. I was all up and ready to buy her this new model medical exoskeleton." He frowned. "I read about it online. It's got all sorts of cool backup voice commands and whatnot, make her stronger and all that, but she refused when I told her about the idea. She said to me she didn't need some fancy gadget to get around, and she'd sooner die than turn into a robot woman. Can you believe that? Guess I should just be happy she can still see all right."

James chuckled. "She's managed to live this long. She must know what she's doing."

"Yeah, that's what I'm thinking, too. In all seriousness, I know she's gonna join the good Lord sooner rather than later, but I think she'll stick around longer than any of us expect." Trey leaned forward, a curious glint in his eye. "Hey, big man, while you're in town, maybe you want to help a brother out?"

"What do you mean?"

"We've got a line on a group of level fours—four of them, funnily enough." Trey shrugged. "Wizards, not normal bounties. I thought it might be interesting to have you tag along since they are special cases."

"How are they not normal bounties?" James replied.

*Here it comes.*

James' gaze dipped to his shirt. His amulet lay concealed, Whispy separated from his chest by a metal spacer. The symbiont might get his first workout in months.

"You heard of Ultimate?" Trey raised an eyebrow.

"Isn't that when stoner college kids play frisbee golf?"

Trey snickered. "Nah. Ultimate is a new drug."

"I haven't heard of it." James shook his head. "Should I have?"

"I mentioned it in some of my reports." Trey sounded amused, not annoyed.

"I don't pay much attention to the day-to-day stuff at the agency anymore. I figure if there's any problems, Maria, Chris, you, or Charlyce will let me know. The last time I was on the move, it was because the government specifically whined at me until I helped them out, but I'm supposed to be retired."

Trey snickered. "Yeah, yeah, I know. Just saying. Anyway, it's new, and I'm talking super-new. I hadn't heard anything about it until a month ago. It's some sort of magical drug, and I don't mean magic-derived like dust or some of those tripping spells." His expression darkened. "Word is it can enhance your magical power in a major way."

James snorted. "Magical steroids?"

"Something like that, yeah." Trey reached into his jacket, pulled out his phone, and tapped it. "The thing is, it's a big gamble as well since it can screw you up. Unpredictable side effects. It can change people, or it can straight-up kill them, and not just because it's not pure. The same part of it that helps charge people up can tear them down."

James furrowed his brow. "And people are actually using it?"

Trey nodded. "In a big way. The thing is, if it does work, someone who might be a level-four bounty can end up a level-five in terms of power. Luckily, it only works if you're already magical, so it's not like street punks are suddenly turning into Brownstone bait, but lame wizards who might have been nothing but enforcers for some local gang have a chance at becoming major players now." He set his phone down and flipped it around. A map of Texas was displayed on the phone with several red dots clustered in the major cities. "It first appeared in Dallas about a month ago. Rumors at first, but the cops and local bounty hunters had a rough time with fools they shouldn't have and found some of it after killing the Ultimate-enhanced wizards in a big shootout. That was when people realized it wasn't a stupid street rumor, and the Feds confirmed it—DEA, the FBI, and PDA. The government's looking into it now in a big way. Not like anyone wants this kind of thing flooding the streets. Too many damned fools out there are willing to take the risk, and the average wizard is already dangerous enough."

James grunted. "And your wizard bounties? They're all into Ultimate?"

"All of them are users, according to my informants." Trey furrowed his brow. "Nobody at the agency has run into anyone we think is a user, but a few other bounty hunters have. Far as I've heard, no Ultimate's hit LA. Probably because of the Brownstone Effect." He scoffed. "They might be able to make enough noise to take down a few of our people there, but if they do that, everyone knows you'll be coming, so they don't bother."

James nodded slowly. Not only was that true, but LA's organized crime families tended to pass along tips about anyone dangerous rolling into town. Everyone preferred the status quo, and everyone likewise understood that if James Brownstone came out of retirement, lots of criminals might end up dead, their buildings destroyed and their organizations annihilated. People had finally learned their lesson.

"So you want me to kick these guys' asses?" James asked. "You think you'll have trouble handling them?"

Trey grimaced. "Nah, nah. We can handle the guys, and I know this is beneath you, but it'd be a nice treat for some of the local guys. Some of these newer dudes have never seen you in action other than grilling. There was just that one level-five back in January. It's inspirational, you know what I'm saying? Hell, I want to see it since it has been a while for me. Plus, if we can get a quick line on where they got their Ultimate, we might be able to stop it before it spreads too far, and make things more pleasant for everyone in Vegas. Cops haven't gotten any leads. Everyone they've dealt with has ended up dead."

James resisted a snort. Trey was a good leader, but even after all these years, he had trouble publicly admitting when he might be outclassed. He always conveniently had an excuse about new hires or morale.

"I'm on a schedule to get to Denver in time for the opening of the restaurant," James explained. "I'm not saying I won't help, but I can't sit around in Las Vegas for a week waiting for the bounties to show up."

Trey waved a hand. "No thing. No thing at all, big man. We've already got a line on these four, and we should have their location pinned down by tomorrow morning. You can stick around until then, right?"

"Sure." James picked up a rib and pointed it as if it were a gun. "But you better have these guys' location. This is supposed to be a vacation and a road trip. I shouldn't have to go making calls."

"You just fill up on barbeque and leave all the hunting to Old Trey over here." The younger man grinned. "Just bring your pain tomorrow. Nothing but the fun part, right?"

James grunted.

*Sure, the fun part.*

## CHAPTER SIX

T he next morning, James snorted from the driver's seat of his F-350 as they headed down the street. "You've got to be fucking kidding me. Seriously?"

Trey laughed from the passenger seat, his phone in his hand. "I swear to the Lord in Heaven. Our drones tagged the guys at long range at the Las Vegas Golf Club. They're hitting the links."

"Your big, bad-ass magical steroid-using wizards are out playing golf?"

"Yeah. So?"

James grunted. "I fucking hate golf."

"It's not like you really like any sport, big man." Trey shrugged. "I'll admit I've been getting into it lately. It's a skill game, but also relaxing. You should give it a try."

"Hitting a ball into a tiny hole," James rumbled. "What's the point?"

"Fun and satisfaction. Just like barbeque."

James shook his head. "Barbeque and golf are two totally different things."

Trey smirked. "Sure. Just saying, we all got our hobbies."

His phone chimed with a message.

James nodded at the phone. "That the team? They golfing, too?"

Trey tapped in a quick response. "We don't have to play golf. We just have to capture our boys. From what our drones show, they just started their game, so we've got plenty of time. Victoria and Ramon are on the way. Since we've got you, we're only bringing four other guys with anti-magic deflectors and anti-magic bullets."

James had worked with the witch Victoria on occasion, but Ramon had been hired years after James' retirement. Although they'd talked several times, he'd never worked with the wizard on an actual job.

"I forgot to ask," James began. "Dead or alive?"

Trey nodded. "Nope. Even though these bastards tore up the local cops in Fort Worth a few weeks ago. I think the cops want to pump them for information."

"AET? I've been pretty lucky about AET teams not being irritated with me in the last few years. There was that shit in Atlanta, but it got cleared up eventually." James growled in frustration.

Trey shook his head. "AET will be on site, but they won't be going after them. Since this is a public place, Vic is calling ahead, but under their current lieutenant, they're always more than willing to let us handle it." He tapped in another message. "Outsourcing the risk."

James turned hard at an intersection, his hands tight on the wheel. "In that case, I know where this golf course is, so let's just meet everyone there and get this over with."

Even as he complained, a thought bubbled up. He couldn't deny the truth.

*It was good to get a little exercise.*

---

As James drove up the road toward the parking lot, he glanced to his right and frowned. "Are they clearing out that school?"

Car after car zoomed past him going the opposite way. Several people were running on foot along the road, panic on their faces.

Trey nodded. "Remember it's a Saturday. They got cops over there too, checking to make sure it's empty. We just need to concentrate on taking down the bounties. If we keep them on the course, no one will get hurt who doesn't have it coming."

"And what about the bounties? There's no way they haven't noticed all the drones in the sky or the red and blue lights?" James nodded toward the approaching parking lot. Police vehicles and officers filled it, including several AET team members with exoskeletons and a mixture of rail-guns, stun rifles, and rocket launchers.

James didn't think about it much, but when he'd started his bounty hunting career, armor and nice rifles were top-of-the-line AET equipment. Now most city's AET teams had exoskeletons or even power armor. Tech might have stagnated when the gates to Oriceran had opened, but humanity's ingenuity could only be held back, never stopped entirely.

*I bet these guys could take these wizards, but they've gotten so used to the agency doing shit that they're willing to be nothing but glorified crowd control. Not sure that's a good thing, but we better take care of this shit quickly.*

James pulled into an open parking spot. Six men and women in dark suits walked toward him, all Brownstone Agency bounty hunters. A pale, short-haired woman with bright red eyes led the pack, her glowing protective glyphs covering her suit and a slender golden rod in her hand. Victoria Stone.

Ramon walked beside her, an easy smile on his face. The man was always smiling. It annoyed James at times, but it wasn't like he had to work with him, and Trey had nothing but good things to say about the wizard.

James and Trey stepped out of his truck. James removed the spacer and gritted his teeth as Whispy's tendrils dug into his chest.

*Initiation,* Whispy sent. *Who are we going to kill today?*

James grunted. When he first understood Whispy, he'd always assumed the symbiont would sound like a computer, but he'd noticed a few months after the Battle of LA that the symbiont's mental personality was slowly changing. Claiming Whispy was becoming more human might be a stretch, but he was becoming something other than a machine obsessed with his former primary directive.

*Four wizards using some sort of enhancement drug,* James sent.

*Unlikely the enemy will present a significant threat or opportunity for adaptation. Kill them quickly. Do not waste time.*

*Not killing them. We need to take them alive. We need information from them.*

*Inefficient use of resources. Your time to waste.*

Trey reached into his pocket and pulled out a small receiver, which he slipped into his ear.

Victoria and the others stopped, and she nodded to James. "Well, if *he's* here, this ought to be quick. I almost feel sorry for those bastards."

James shrugged. "I could just watch."

The men around her looked disappointed.

"Nothing wrong with things being quick." Victoria frowned and jerked her head toward Trey.

Trey nodded and tapped his receiver, an annoyed look on his face.

James looked between them. "What's going on?"

"The bounties finally seem to care that people are here," Trey explained. "Two of them are breaking away from the others." He squinted into the distance. "How about this? Me, Vic, and Ramon go after two, and James goes after the other two? That way we can clean this up before too much happens." He gestured to the other four bounty hunters. "Y'all stay here as backup in case they get past us. If they do, that means we screwed up, and they're too dangerous. Take them down in that case. Don't worry about the money. We don't want the cops thinking we can't handle our business."

The bounty hunters nodded.

James nodded. "Fine by me." From his pocket, he pulled out a small ring. "Glad I have a suitcase filled with clothes." He reached under his shirt and placed the ring against his amulet. It was time for a Shay treat.

Most people would never get access to a magical arti-fact of even moderate power, but he always kept a few on him to feed Whispy. Even though he had a better connection with his symbiont than he'd had in the past, they still hadn't figured out a good way to hit extended advanced mode other than feeding on magic or being pissed off, and it was hard to care much about a semi-routine bounty.

*Let's do this shit,* James sent.

*Draining alternate power source,* Whispy responded. *Sufficient power for extended advanced transformation.*

The ring crumbled to dust and silver-green metallic tendrils spread over James' body, solidifying into a layer of biometallic armor. His armor's expansion shredded his poor pants and shirt. Claws sprang from his covered hands, and two blades grew from the tops of his arms.

A helmet enclosed his head, and darkness took over for a moment before his new expanded range of vision kicked in.

"Let's make this quick," James rumbled. "What direction are the guys I need to go after headed in?"

Trey pointed to the north, past the sandy-brown clubhouse building adjoining the parking lot.

"I'm gonna let you finish off your guys." James crouched and leapt into the air.

A little height helped James spot two of the wizards in the distance before he landed. A few more mighty bounds put him in front of the two men. They didn't bother to shoot at him as he flew through the air.

Both wizards wore khaki pants and short-sleeved polo shirts, sufficient for the slightly chilly high fifties temperatures. Their golf bags were slung over their shoulders. If it weren't for the wands poking out of their bags, they might look like normal men who wanted to hit a few holes on the weekend.

One man's face twitched and his veins pulsed with light.

*Yeah, that's not normal,* James thought. *Not that I'm one to talk.*

*Unlikely enemy will present significant threat,* Whispy sent, weariness underlying the thought.

The two bounties dropped their bags and yanked their wands out.

The twitching man with the colorful veins glared at James. "Why are you of all people fucking here?"

James grinned. "Good, you recognize me. That makes shit simple. If you recognize me, then you know what I can do."

The man's eyes bulged. "Yes, I recognize you, Brownstone. But why the fuck are you here?"

James grunted. "Because you fuckers have bounties."

"You're coming after level fours now?" The man's eyes started glowing, and his skin began to bubble. "I know you did that shit in January, but those guys weren't level fours."

*Even target acknowledges it is an insignificant threat,* Whispy sent.

*That just means this won't take long.*

The wizard's partner frowned and shook his head. "I said you shouldn't have used so much. It's fucking you up."

"So you're doing Ultimate?" James asked. "That shit isn't gonna help you win against me, and it sounds like you already know that. You're messing yourself up for no good reason."

"I was having the best fucking game of my life," the

mutating wizard screamed. "Fucking PGA-Tour good! And now you're here screwing with me." He cut through the air with his wand. "I just wanted to relax."

"So did a lot of the people you've killed." James shrugged. "You could make this shit easy on yourself."

The man's head jerked violently back and forth as patches of bubbling skin solidified into hard, reflective patches of black, like he was coating himself with obsidian. "Ultimate has changed everything. You know what? Fuck you. I'm not the man I once was."

*Destroy the enemy who lacks facial symmetry first,* Whispy suggested.

*Why? You think he's tougher?*

*His statements grow wearying.*

James snickered at Whispy before nodding at the wizard. "Yeah, I see it changed you. You're one ugly motherfucker."

"You're one to talk, Brownstone." The mutating wizard looked at his partner. "You planning on surrendering?"

The normal wizard lifted his wand and shook his head. "We can win. We've got Ultimate on our side, and you've got to be more powerful with all the shit I'm seeing."

The mutating wizard turned back to James. His eyes had turned solid black. His skin stopped changing, but a dull blue light illuminated his surface blood vessels. "Power, Brownstone. You didn't really think you would win forever? Isn't that why you ran off to your restaurant?"

James snorted. "You really have no fucking clue, do you?"

*His statements grow extremely wearying,* Whispy complained. *Eliminate target.*

*I need to keep him alive,* James sent.

*Then cripple target.*

James grunted and retracted his blades. It was too easy to accidentally kill someone when he was swinging the weapons, let alone if he decided to use an energy attack. It was time for a good old-fashioned beatdown. Breaking a few things would still leave the men on the "alive" end of the dead-or-alive spectrum.

The mutant wizard pointed his wand and screamed an incantation. Three different glyphs appeared in front of him and lines of red energy flowed among them, humming with power.

The normal wizard opted for a more straightforward fireball. His spell exploded around James, barely singeing his armor. Charred grass and dirt shot up around him.

*Maximum adaptation already achieved,* Whispy complained.

"Nice try, but you're gonna have to do better than that," James growled. He leapt toward the normal wizard and brought his armored fist down, but his blow bounced off an invisible shield.

James expected the defense, but that didn't make it less annoying.

The fireball wizard grinned. "You can't hit what you can't touch. Yeah, we'll win. Maybe you should be the one running, Brownstone."

James uncurled his fingers and swiped at the man's chest with his claws. His first blow bounced off, but the second passed deeper, slowed but not stopped, ripping into the man's shirt and drawing blood.

With a yelp, the wizard backpedaled before firing off another quick fireball, and then another.

James marched forward, ignoring the other man, who was channeling energy into his attack. He was in no hurry, and no one was running anymore. He made another fist and slammed it into the chest of the now-shieldless wizard.

There was an audible crunch, and the man screamed. He flew a dozen yards and landed on his back in a nearby sand trap, coughing up blood. His wand lay several feet away.

"You broke my fucking ribs!" the wizard screamed.

"You're still alive," James growled, "so stop bitching." He turned to his partner. The bright glyphs were nearly blinding, but James didn't activate a visual filter. "Give it up, asshole. Some weak-ass drug doesn't mean you can win against me. You'd need to take all the Ultimate in the world to have a chance against me."

"I'll make sure everyone knows those were your last words," the mutant wizard snarled. Three rays of energy burst from the glyphs and converged on a single point to grow a pulsating translucent sphere of scarlet energy. James didn't bother to dodge as the wizard released the attack.

The massive explosion blinded James and sent him careening through the air. He crashed into a nearby putting green, leaving a huge indentation. Flaming debris rocks and dirt showered down around him as he hopped to his feet.

*I feel sorry for the groundskeeper,* James thought.

*Minimum damage sustained,* Whispy reported. *Maximum*

*adaptation already achieved. Eliminate target. End this ineffi-*
*cient battle.*

James grunted. He wasn't in pain, and his armor was already repairing what little surface damage he had sustained. Facing a level five taking Ultimate might present a challenge, but these two wizards were just punks standing between him and more barbeque.

"I'm still here, asshole," James called.

The wizard's face twitched. "That's not my only trick." He growled and pointed his wand again.

A chain appeared and shot toward James. He swiped with his claws, separating it into two halves.

James scoffed, the filter of the helmet giving it a hollow sound. "Please. That's your big plan?"

With wide eyes, the wizard stumbled backward, his wand still up. An earthen wall shot from the ground and James leapt over it with ease, landing on the opposite side of the now-fleeing mutant wizard.

The man stumbled to a halt, his lip quivering.

"What's the matter?" James rumbled. "You talked all that shit and now you're running away? Why don't you show me what a badass you are, Mr. Ultimate? I don't know if all that shit on your body is permanent, but if it is, it's a high price to pay when you're still gonna get your ass kicked."

Two quick blows from James sent the wizard into his earthen wall. The wizard's magic protected him, but he stumbled and dropped his wand.

*End this inefficient battle,* Whispy demanded

*Yeah, fair enough. Just wanted to talk a little trash first.*

*Trash-talking is inefficient use of resources.*

James extended a blade and thrust forward, cutting

through the shield and pinning the bounty against the wall. The mutated man howled in pain before James knocked him out with a punch. He pulled his blade out and the man fell to the ground.

"I hope you didn't spend too much on your drugs," James muttered. He frowned and looked toward where he'd been standing when he was attacked. Smoke rose from a massive crater that could have easily swallowed his truck. "Huh. That *is* halfway impressive when I look at it from here. Too bad you were up against me."

James peered through the smoky battleground. Trey and the team could handle the other two men.

# CHAPTER SEVEN

As soon as James had jumped away, Trey, Victoria, and Ramon charged across the course after their targets. Trey already had his magic gloves and tie on, and Victoria and Ramon had been ready since their arrival at the golf course.

Police helicopters circled overhead, along with drones. The police were prepared for the Brownstone Agency's team to take the first crack at the criminals, but they weren't prepared to let anyone get away. Trey wasn't worried. There was no way they would lose, and even if by some miracle they did, the wizards would be so busted up, the backup team would be able to take them down.

Trey laughed as they closed on two figures rushing toward them.

Victoria glanced at him. "What's so funny?"

"I asked the big man to help so other people could see him in action, but now we're off fighting separately." Trey shrugged. "Not the end of the world, but still kind of funny."

Ramon chuckled. "Yeah, that's true, but at least we have him as backup if we need him. I'm sure he won't have any trouble with the two he's facing off against. We better not end up looking like fools."

Trey shook his head. "Nah. We got this."

Victoria dropped from a run to a jog as the two wizards approached. Human-shaped piles of dirt flanked them on either side. The dirt-men lacked any obvious eyes.

Ramon frowned. "What are those?"

"I'm thinking it's kind of like May's specialty," Trey offered. "Except they're doing it with dirt instead of statues." He sighed and shook his head. "It's not as satisfying beating down those kinds of things."

"I never did care much for that kind of magic."

The wizards and their makeshift army walked toward the bounty hunters, the two bounties grinning from ear to ear.

"They look sure of themselves," Trey offered.

"That'll make this more satisfying," Victoria responded.

The roar of fireballs sounded in the distance.

"Sounds like the big man is getting into it," Trey muttered. "We better get to it, too." He shook his head. "We're with the Brownstone Agency," he shouted. "You have level-four bounties on you for a list of crimes so long I don't even feel like mentioning all of them, so why don't you just be nice about this and surrender? You're done, boys. Don't waste our time and yours."

"Bounty-hunter scum," one of the wizards called, a tall thin man who contrasted with his stout partner. "You have no idea who you're facing. You think we're afraid of you?"

Trey adjusted his tie. "I definitely know who I'm facing,

but the question is, do you? If you did, then yeah, you'd damned well be afraid."

A massive boom shook the area. Everyone, including the wizards, glanced into the distance to see the rising plume of dirt and smoke.

The thin wizard snickered. "Whatever other team you had is already dead. I'm just trying to decide how much we should toy with you before we kill you."

Trey laughed. "Really, fool? You think our other team is dead? Do you know who that other team is?"

"A bunch of corpses?" The wizard shrugged. "I don't care."

Trey gave him a wide grin, his eyes filled with amusement. "Nah. James Brownstone in the flesh. Armored flesh, but still the flesh. Even if by some tiny chance you get by us, and by some tiny chance you get by our backup, and by some miniscule chance you get by the AET, you really think you're gonna escape the Granite Ghost?" He laughed. "If you do, you're dumber than I thought."

Fear flashed across the wizard's face before resignation crept in to replace it. "James Brownstone's just a man who ran away from bounty hunting. It won't matter to you if he catches us or not, because you'll be dead soon." He pointed his wand and the dirt-men charged, their collective movement fueling a cacophony of soft thuds.

Trey snorted. "Let's do it hard, then."

Victoria pointed her wand and chanted a spell. A golden blast blew off the head of a dirt-man and it collapsed into a normal pile of dirt and rock. She took down another.

Ramon flourished his wand with a big grin before

shouting his own incantation. A blue-white bolt of lightning crackled from the wand, striking one dirt-man before arcing to two more. The first target fell to the ground. The other two continued forward, only slightly slowed, blackened holes in them.

More rose from the ground at the chant of the thin wizard.

Trey wasn't about to waste anti-magic bullets on a bunch of dirt piles, but there were too many of the damned things between him and the wizards.

Victoria and Ramon continued firing, downing the advancing army. Trey took his chance and sprinted to the side. If he could flank the wizards and get close, he could use his gloves. They granted him strength, and Zoe had increased their offensive and defensive power through the years, but they still required him to be able to land a punch.

A squad of dirt-men broke away from the main army to charge him. Their run was more a jog than a sprint, but their sheer numbers ensured his surprise attack from the rear strategy was doomed.

Trey growled in frustration and met the first dirt-man with a solid punch through its head. His opponent collapsed into its components. A kick sent another one to the ground but didn't finish it off. His punch through the chest of third dirt-man wasn't any more effective, so Trey followed up with a hook that knocked its head off.

"At least I know where we have to hit," Trey muttered.

A few of Trey's foes got in hits of their own. The powerful blows stung, but they failed to bring down the magical shield emanating from his gloves and a recent anniversary gift, his otherwise-unassuming silk tie. There were a lot of perks that came from being married to a powerful witch.

His partners continued to keep their distance from the army, their magical attacks finishing enemies off without risk.

A flurry of punches from Trey sent more of the enemy into piles, but new enemies kept growing from the ground closer to the wizards.

Trey glanced toward the bounties and frowned. A problem had arisen that wasn't made of dirt. "Yo, I only see one guy," he murmured. He didn't need to be loud since the field team all had comm gear, with the exception of James. "Backup team, be ready in case he's coming your way."

"Will do, Trey," the backup team replied over the comm in unison.

"Same here," Victoria replied quietly through the receiver. "I don't know when I lost him. Ramon?"

"Crap," the wizard replied. "I was too focused on Mr. Clean's nightmare army." He punctuated his sentence with another blast into the enemy.

Trey downed a few more dirt-men and sprinted a few yards away. Ultimate-enhanced wizards didn't disappear without reason. Maybe the bastard had decided to let his friend take all the heat once he saw that the bounty hunters weren't afraid of the dirt-man army.

"Not only that, these guys are endless," Trey complained. "Even if they're easy to beat. If these wizards were normal, I'd say they'd run out of juice, but who knows how long they can keep going with the Ultimate?"

"Ramon, cover me," Victoria replied. "I'm going to

charge up and carve a path through." She began a rapid chant.

"Okay." Ramon followed up with two quicker but less powerful lightning blasts, but each was sufficient to down enemies.

While Trey respected the flexibility and power spells brought to a battle, there was something satisfying and straightforward about just shooting or punching someone. He didn't need to think to use his artifacts. He just needed to fight.

Trey refocused on the horde trying to take him down. Victoria and Ramon could handle their own trouble. He needed to either get through the horde or come up with a new and better plan.

After destroying a few more dirt-men, Trey spotted a small hole in their formation closer to his side. He grinned to himself.

"I think I spotted our boy," Trey whispered while decapitating another animate pile of earth. "Or at least where I think he is. Just need a distraction." A bright golden glow caught his attention out of the corner of his eye, and he jumped back and glanced that way.

A dozen glyphs inscribed in a circle of cerulean light floated in front of the chanting Victoria. Trey had seen this spell before.

"Yeah, that would make for a nice distraction."

Victoria shouted the last part of her spell, and scores of golden orbs burst from the glyphs and showered the dirt-man army. Explosions ripped up the ground as they obliterated the magical creations, knocking them back into nothing more than the common dust and rock. Dust to dust, indeed.

Trey laughed as he realized they might not clear much of a profit on the job after they got done paying for all the damage to the golf course.

The witch's rain of golden death continued. It blew a wide hole in the enemy line and knocked the wizard controlling it to the ground, groaning and half-burned. The army swayed in place, now easy targets for Ramon. Victoria fell to one knee and took a deep breath.

Trey charged into the survivors closer to him. Many of them hadn't been hit by Victoria's barrage, and the opening he had spotted earlier remained. He shoved and punched the dirt-men out of the way as he closed on the opening, his hand reaching inside his jacket.

The other wizard shimmered into existence as Trey finished pulling his gun out of his pocket. Trey lowered his aim and squeezed off several quick shots.

The sneer on the bounty's face disappeared when the anti-magic bullets weren't deflected by his shield. They were slowed, but the three-shot cluster still managed to clip him in the leg. The wizard grimaced and stumbled to the side, bleeding.

Trey finished his approach and jumped into the air, cocking his other fist back. He slammed his enchanted glove hard against the head of the shielded wizard, and the man flew backward with a grunt and crashed into a couple of the dirt-men.

Before the groaning wizard could rise, Trey marched over to him and knelt, his gun pointed right at him. "I don't want to waste the money shooting you with my expensive-ass bullets, but I will if I have to."

The wizard's hand flexed, but his wand was out of reach. He groaned and let his head fall back. "I can't believe it turned out this way. The Ultimate was supposed to make us unbeatable."

Trey shrugged. "Don't screw with the Brownstone Agency and you won't end up messed up."

The thin wizard passed out, and the dirt-men began falling to the ground in chunks.

Trey narrowed his eyes and smirked at the bleeding wizard. "I've read about you. You aren't major players. You had to get your Ultimate from somewhere, and you just suddenly show up and figure you're all that." He grinned. It was time to go all in on OG Trey. "I don't give two shits about you stonewalling the cops, but you're gonna tell me right now where you got that Ultimate."

The wizard spat. "I'm not telling you shit, bounty hunter."

A shadow passed overhead, and the armored James landed about ten yards away.

Trey nodded toward him. "You want to tell the big man there, don't you?" He stood and holstered his gun. "Because who knows what'll happen if he gets pissed off? Maybe I'll tell him you insulted his daughter," he murmured.

"I didn't say shit about his daughter." The wizard glared at Trey.

Trey grinned. "I didn't say you did. I just said I'd tell him you did."

The wizard swallowed. "Boris Egorov."

Trey laughed. "Now, that wasn't so hard."

# CHAPTER EIGHT

Trey leaned against James' truck as armed police loaded the wounded bounties into separate ambulances. James remained in his armor, his helmet retracted. Shay had extracted a promise about public nudity after a few other high-profile fights, and he didn't want to open his suitcase yet and fish out clothes.

Whispy had gone quiescent after whining about inefficiency. James wondered if that meant a well-timed attack might harm him more than usual, but the situation was well in hand.

James spotted anti-magic emitters set up in the back of the ambulances and narrowed his eyes. The first time he'd heard of the newer devices was after someone had tried to use them on Alison and one of her friends. That little test had ended with Alison and her friends taking down the men trying to ambush her since they'd failed to remember that she didn't only have magic to rely on.

*Guess those anti-magic things don't matter much now since*

*they have to be in a small area, but what happens in fifty years? Will they even need bounty hunters in fifty years if they have shit like that but better?*

James shook his head. It didn't matter. It wouldn't be his problem. He wasn't even supposed to be working this job. His favor had turned complicated, and he needed to get back on the road soon.

"Do the cops need anything else from me?" James asked.

Trey shook his head. "Not that I've heard."

"I should probably get going, then."

"Maybe, but hear me out." Trey moved away from the truck. "I got that name—Boris Egorov—from the bounty."

James nodded. "Yeah, what about him? He's the Ultimate dealer?"

"Way more than that." Trey glanced back and forth and lowered his voice. "Egorov is Russian Mafia. He used to hang in, get this, Dallas until a couple of months ago. He's a smart guy. He knows enough to keep his hands clean, so no bounties, but I've been hearing rumors that he's making a big play. I hadn't connected him with Ultimate because the word on the street was that drugs weren't his game. He's supposed to be a big arms dealer. Some people even say he's got a few big politicians in his pocket."

James frowned. "Sounds like a piece of shit, but you just said he didn't have a bounty. No bounty means it's not your problem. It's not like it's cheap to run the agency or keep you guys in gear. Just because I don't pay much attention doesn't mean that changes."

Trey raised a hand. "Sure, sure. I feel you, big man, but if this guy's bringing in Ultimate into Las Vegas, he's making problems for the agency, even if those problems don't appear until later. The guys we took down today weren't all that, but what happens if some Ultimate freak decides to go to the Strip or Fremont Street and make a point by killing a bunch of people? And who knows if that side-effect stuff makes them go crazy? If AET had taken these guys on, it might not have gone as well." He lowered his hand. "I get that we're not the cops, and I get that we can't go around trying to solve everyone's problems, but we both know you've taken on plenty of ass-kickings that weren't exactly profitable."

James grunted. "I had my reasons, and those usually involved self-defense."

"Yeah, big man. *Usually.*" Trey smirked. "Sometimes you just decided to stop some bastard because they had it coming, even if the money wasn't all lined up right away."

"What are you saying, then?" James furrowed his brow. Everything Trey had said was true, even if James didn't like it.

"I'm saying we go take out Egorov." Trey pointed to one of the ambulances as it pulled away. "That way, three months from now this city's not flooded with level fives blowing up casinos and killing people. Sure, the agency and cops can take them down, but that's only if we see them coming. And even though we've got a little Brownstone Effect here, it's not as strong as it is in LA. Sometimes I think scumbags are coming here to test out if they're ready for LA."

James folded his arms over his chest. "It's a waste of time. If you're not gonna get paid, you're just burning cash and supplies. Turn the name over to the cops and let them do their thing. You're a bounty hunter, not a cop." He nodded toward a few uniformed officers in the distance. "They've got AET. If they have surprise, they can take this Egorov down."

"Come on, big man. You know how it goes. Cops have restraints. They'll have to do surveillance and build up a case. They can't go knocking on the man's door without a lot of paperwork, and having some piece-of-garbage bounty throw Egorov's name out isn't gonna be enough for them to move quickly. By the time they get going, it might be too late. Ultimate could be all over the city." Trey's phone chimed, and he pulled it out and smiled. He shook the device. "The city's already paying for the four we just took down. That's nice. Maybe the golf course will cut us a break on the damage. They've got to have insurance."

The agency's feeble attempts to maintain their own insurance had failed years ago. Everyone respected the Brownstone Agency's ability to take down bounties, but everyone also understood that like their eponymous founder, the men and women now staffing the agency couldn't always accomplish that without a decent amount of collateral damage. There wasn't an insurance provider on either planet who could make giving them a policy profitable.

James surveyed the golf course. Dark wisps of smoke lingered in the air, but from a distance, a person couldn't make out much damage. There were only a few major craters, so it might not end up being as expensive to repair the course. The bounty hunters hadn't even blown up any buildings, and that already made the battle less destructive than James' last little exercise session with the agency.

He couldn't help but be reminded of the utter destruction of a USC baseball field that had occurred during the Battle of LA. The actual number of damaged sporting areas over the course of his career had been low. Most bounties and crazed enemies didn't hang out on golf courses or baseball fields.

*I should sit down and figure out how many mansions, warehouses, and labs I have blown up throughout my career.*

James chuckled.

Trey eyed him. "Is that a good laugh or a bad laugh?"

"Don't worry about it." James locked eyes with Trey. "It also doesn't change how I feel about Egorov and doing shit for free. It sets up a bad precedent. It'd be one thing if Egorov threatened you. Self-defense is good for the reputation."

*I wonder how often they're doing that kind of thing for free? Maybe I shouldn't be bitching since the agency is still profitable. If I want to run shit, I should run shit. Trey and the others have done a good job since I stepped away.*

Trey took a deep breath. "Egorov might not have a bounty, but he's surrounded by guys who do. If we raid his place, we're guaranteed to snatch more than a few guys with bounties while making our lives easier and the city safer in the long run." He shrugged. "And that's saying the cops don't find us a convenient retroactive bounty for Egorov. You know how they are when it comes to this kind of guy, especially in Vegas. Hell, at this point, we're pretty much the primary private AET for them, and they've said as much several times."

James sighed and shook his head. It annoyed him, but he was losing the argument. "I'm supposed to be taking a slow and relaxing road trip to Denver, and now I'm gonna help take down some mob boss whose place is probably surrounded by guys on Ultimate?"

Trey laughed. "Come on, those fools don't stress you out. You can't tell me they do, and Egorov doesn't have a lot of magicals. He's smart enough to not surround himself with freaky mutants. Like I said, arms dealer. I'm thinking our boy is gonna have military-grade weapons." He nodded toward an AET officer in an exoskeleton standing in front of a police van. "I'm thinking it won't be as easy to take him down. Sometimes I like taking on magicals more than normal dudes, because magicals get cocky and forget there is always a way to get through a power."

"I'm not stressed about them. I'm just worried about my trip." James' gaze scanned the police and the other bounty hunters, who were standing around chatting. "I'm already a day behind schedule. Is this gonna take a long time? I don't want to sit around in Vegas waiting for you to corner some mobster unless he's hiding out in some kick-ass barbeque place I don't know about."

Trey shook his head. "I've got you covered, big man. We already know where Egorov is. Since we already had our eye on him, we went through the trouble of scoping out his headquarters a few weeks ago. We can just knock down his door and knock his ass out, and you can be on your way. Ain't no big thing. Once we take out Egorov and his boys, the cops can do their thing, and you can get back on the road." He shrugged. "I'm not saying we can't handle the guy without you, but you do have a way of making things less complicated."

James rubbed the back of his neck and sighed. "Fine. If you already know where he is, we might as well get this shit over with."

Trey offered him a bright smile. "Great. Thanks, big man. You're making the rest of my year easier."

CHAPTER NINE

An hour later, a line of vans, trucks, and SUVs all pulled up in front of a large fenced mansion and parked. Several Brownstone Agency drones circled high overhead as the bounty hunters hopped out of their vehicles, all in tactical vests layered over their chest armor. Everyone was equipped with a rifle and a stun rod, along with multiple sonic grenades and flashbangs.

James frowned and looked around, his helmet back on and his armor recharged with the help of another Shay treat. He didn't see any obvious guards around the mansion. His instincts suggested that meant Egorov knew they were coming and fled, but Trey had told him they'd been watching the mansion, and no one had arrived or left in the last hour.

Trey pointed into the air and circled with his hand. "Everyone but the primary entry team, continue surrounding the place. No one's running yet, but they might get a little less brave once their guys start going down."

Other Brownstone vehicles were unloading on different sides of the mansion. Everyone was linked via comm except James, who'd turned down the offer of a receiver. It felt too much like work. This was just a favor for a friend.

"If he's not gone, then this shit's probably a trap," James rumbled.

Trey shrugged. "I'm sure our boy has a few nice toys, but that's why we brought you along."

"I'm a nice toy?" James snorted.

"You're the nicest toy, big man." Trey offered him a merry smile. "Just a little dangerous, is all."

Victoria and Ramon jogged over to Trey. "The specialists are all in position."

Trey had ordered some of the other magicals working in Vegas to spread out with the other teams. He didn't want to leave any holes in the defenses.

*Good idea,* James thought. He had to admit that the people running the agency now were better at that type of planning. Even when he was directly involved, his strategy had mostly consisted of kicking the enemy's ass quickly enough that none of his guys would be in big trouble.

Trey pointed to the gate. "Let's go say hello."

Victoria, Trey, Ramon, and James marched toward the front gate, which had an intercom pad off to the side.

Trey strode over and pressed the Call button. "Hello, this is Trey Garfield of the Brownstone Agency. We're going to need everyone inside to come out with their hands up. Anyone who doesn't have a bounty will be free to go, but we know there are more than a few men inside with bounties." He released the button. "There we go. Nice, fair warning."

The massive door to the large unattached garage off to the side groaned and lifted, and the front double doors flew open. A man in power armor clanked out, a rocket launcher in one arm and a heavy machine gun in the other. The device was an evolution over a mere exoskeleton. The clunky form could easily be mistaken for a robot, but a human was inside operating the machine. Anti-magic deflector crystals were embedded in the upper chest portion of the armor.

Two additional soldiers in power armor emerged from the garage.

James narrowed his eyes. "More complicated shit—Ultimate and power armor. No one is just a mobster anymore with a magic sword?" He scoffed.

"Got three armors up front," Trey reported over the comm with a frown. "Support, make sure none are sneaking around back." He turned to James. "That's a little more gear than we planned on. Ultimate dealing's apparently damned profitable." He snorted. "Wait. Shit. I know who these guys are. We got a report about a merc company sniffing around Vegas looking for work. They weren't supposed to be coming in for a few days. Good news is, the whole company has a bounty on them, and they don't come to America much, so we've already got some decent bounties lined up even if no one else inside has one. Just need to play it careful in case more are hiding."

James shook his head. "I'm sure that's their best play up front. I'll take those assholes out, and everyone else can sweep in after me. I can't have this shit take all day. I need to get back on the road." He jumped into the air before Trey could respond and extended a blade.

The power armor near the front raised its metal-and-polymer arm and opened up with its machine gun, the sound thunderous. A steady stream of shell casings clattered to the cement of the porch as torrents of bullets filled the sky and converged on James. The bullets bounced off his armor, scratching it but not accomplishing much else.

*Maximum adaptation already achieved,* Whispy reported. *Attacks conventional in nature. Further engagement unlikely to yield additional adaptation. Quickly eliminate enemies.*

A rocket hissed away from one of the garage armors toward one of the agency's SUVs and the bounty hunters scattered before the projectile struck. An explosion enveloped the vehicle and threw it into the air. The burning wreck tumbled end over end and almost crushed a fleeing bounty hunter.

*Damn,* James thought, *you're right. I better pick this shit up.*

The agency bounty hunters opened fire.

James grunted as he dropped toward the front porch. While he trusted the agency to take targets down, that didn't mean they would always be able to do it without casualties.

With a mighty thud, James landed in front of the first power-armored opponent. The armor batted at him with a thick arm, but James blocked it with his own, producing a loud clank that sounded like metal hitting metal. His opponent stepped back and fired his rocket into James' chest.

The explosion blinded him for a second and knocked him back a few feet.

*Minimal damage. Armor regeneration in progress,* Whispy reported.

Explosions, the crack of gunfire, and the hiss of stun bolts filled the air. A few fireballs and lightning bolts joined them, but the anti-magic deflectors of the armor weakened the attacks, leaving it blackened and pitted but not seriously damaged.

James swung his blade wide and cut through the machine gun and arm of his opponent. The armored soldier jerked back, and the sparking stump revealed the gloved hand of the human operator inside. A few more inches and James would have taken a trophy. A few quick stabs and slices had the suit staggering backward, its movement rigid, sparking, and smoking.

The helmet and chest of the armor hissed and swung open, revealing a bloodied operator.

*Huh,* James thought. *I went deeper than I thought.*

The operator's shaking hands moved toward the straps that helped keep him inside. James marched toward the other man and laid him out, armor and all, with a single punch that sent him crashing into the foyer of the mansion.

Dozens of men swept with automatic rifles swept around the far walls of the foyer from the front hall of the mansion and opened fire on James. He jumped back and ducked around the wall, not out of fear but because he had another concern: protecting the agency's bounty hunters.

The other two armored men continued to pin most of the bounty hunters with a steady stream of bullets and the occasional rocket. Their anti-magic deflectors darkened, but they were nowhere near black and shattering.

James raised his blade and pointed at one. Green sparks appeared around his blade, leaping across the weapon and increasing in frequency. The suits turned to concentrate their gunfire on him. At least if they were firing at him, they couldn't fire at any of the bounty hunters.

A couple of rockets followed a few seconds later, forcing James back and into a crossfire with the mercenaries in the foyer.

*Maximum adaptation already achieved*, Whispy reported. *Anticipate enemy ammo shortage before significant damage achieved.*

James grunted. Although the bullet storm wasn't hurting him or his armor, the sheer volume of hot lead being slung at him was distracting. He released his own charge, and a green beam blasted from his blade and arm. The attack carved through the first armored suit, a red Maserati in the garage, and the side wall of the garage.

The blast left a smoking hole in the center of the armored suit and its operator and it toppled over.

*Shit. I might have wasted the bounty.*

*Enemy is unlikely to have survived removal of heart and lungs*, Whispy helpfully clarified.

*Thanks for that.*

James crouched as bullets and grenades exploded around him, the attacks showering him with dirt and shrapnel. He would have to close and disable the enemy with his blades and claws or risk another kill, especially after his lecture to Trey about doing things for free.

James' expanded vision might not truly let him see behind him, but it let him see enough. Trey rushed down the street with a grenade launcher, pointed at the surviving suit of armor, and pulled the trigger.

A small silver grenade flew toward the armored merc, popping up with a few blue sparks once it completed its flight. James couldn't hear anything in the overwhelming din of the gunfire and other explosions, but the sparks and arcs of electricity let him know what Trey's plan had been: EMP the bastard.

The suit stopped moving, and a moment later, the back opened instead of the front.

*All sorts of models. Fancy.*

The operator dropped out and laid on his stomach, then put his hands on his head, accepting that he was outclassed.

James turned back toward the foyer. The mercenaries continued their barrages, occasionally swapping out magazines. Given some of the colored bands he saw, James suspected they were using anti-magic rounds and were confused as to why they weren't doing much more than bouncing off him.

Several small grenades flew past James from behind and into the foyer. They didn't explode or spark but gave off high-pitched whines, and the mercenaries fell over, clutching their ears.

James grinned. Trey might have underestimated what Egorov would have to protect himself, but Egorov had also underestimated the type of gear a top-level bounty-hunting agency could bring when they knew they were facing off against an arms dealer.

The bounty hunters began advancing on all sides, jogging forward with wands, stun rifles, regular rifles, and grenade launchers at the ready. No one would be escaping the house now.

James charged inside. The quicker he found Egorov, the sooner he could get back on the road and the safer the other bounty hunters would be. More than a few men in business suits lay groaning among the downed mercenaries. Egorov's crew, he assumed.

*This asshole can't have many more guys left, but I bet he's still got a trick or two.*

James continued into the main hall. The mansion was only one story, but it was wide and deep. He looked back and forth for a few seconds. With the option to go straight, left, or to the right, he decided his best bet was straight.

The heavy thuds of his armored feet echoed through the long, wide hallway as he ran past various vases and paintings. A few pieces of them rattled as he passed and fell to the ground, shattering.

*Hope that shit wasn't too expensive.*

After several turns, other rooms presented themselves, but James ignored them and continued charging toward the golden-leaf double doors at the end of the hallway. A room with such an ostentatious entrance had to be where Egorov was hiding.

James grunted as an invisible force knocked him back with a flash. He shook his head and stood.

*Minimum damage*, Whispy reported. *Maximum adaptation already achieved.*

*Magic?* James asked.

*Energy signature is consistent with previous such exposure.*

James snorted and raised his blade. He stabbed a few times until his blade slid through the air with ease, then sliced back and forth a few more times before stepping forward. While he wasn't sure if he'd carved a piece out of the invisible wall or killed the entire thing, he was able to proceed to the door without any new challenges.

Two more expensive-looking vases painted with ancient Greek scenes rested on square stands on either side. James thought about knocking them down, but if they were ancient artifacts, Shay might be pissed.

He looked over his shoulder and grimaced. A good third of the vases in the hallway had met their end during his lumbering extended-advanced mode stroll, even though he hadn't been purposely trying to knock them over.

*Oh, well. Not like Shay needs to know.*

The gunfire and the hiss of stun bolts echoed down the hallway, along with the clomping of bounty hunters entering the mansion. There were still a few small fish left, but it sounded like Trey and the others had that under control.

James looked the golden doors up and down. They didn't look old, or as if they had been taken from some ancient tomb. They just looked gaudy, so he turned and kicked. With a loud crack, one of the doors flew inward and crashed to the floor.

A dark-haired man with a scar across his cheek sat behind a massive glass desk with nothing on it but a single computer and a rusty ball-peen hammer. Boris Egorov might have had some chance at being intimidating if he hadn't been wearing a white bathrobe, his hair still wet.

"I interrupt your shower?" James rumbled. "Sorry."

*Enemy is unlikely to present significant adaptation potential,* Whispy complained. *Efficiently neutralize and end battle.*

Egorov offered a tight smile. "I have to applaud you, Mr. Brownstone." His voice had only a trace of an accent. "You live up to all the hype. I never imagined you would come after me. Aren't you supposed to be retired?"

James shrugged. "I'm supposed to be on a barbeque road trip, but shit came up. You're a dumbass to be pushing Ultimate in Vegas. You should have stayed away from Vegas and LA. If you had, you might not have had to deal with me."

Several screams and shouts filtered in from the hallway.

James pointed over his shoulder with his clawed hand. "We took out your mercs and your men, and the few assholes remaining won't last long. There's no one left to save you, Egorov."

The robed mobster picked up the hammer and patted the head in his palm. "I'll admit you've inconvenienced me." He raised his hand, on which he wore a silver ring. He twisted the ring, and a shimmering field surrounded him. "But I'm not yet ready to surrender. Let me share a little epiphany with you, Mr. Brownstone."

James narrowed his eyes, wondering what the deal was with the hammer. "What?"

"I followed the trials of those corporate bastards your daughter took out in Seattle," Egorov explained. He stood, and a low hum came from the hammer. "A lot of interesting talk about magicals and normal people. Are we the same? Different?"

"I don't care about any of that shit," James growled.

The footsteps of several bounty hunters, including

Trey, Victoria, and Ramon, sounded behind him.

Egorov nodded. "Good. I agree with you. I came to the same conclusion. Magic isn't power. Not really." He slammed the hammer into the glass table. Glowing cracks shot through it, and a couple seconds later it collapsed to the ground in a heap of shards. "Magic's just a tool. *Money* is power. It was why those rich corporate fuckers could almost stand up to your daughter and her people, even though they had no magical power. And your daughter? Well, she's a Drow princess." The mobster stepped through the glass and it crunched beneath him, the shimmering field around him saving his bare feet from being shredded. "It's why I can have mercs in power armor protecting me, and things like my ring and this hammer." He twisted the hammer in the air. "You like it? I got it a few weeks ago. It's great for making a point when a man disappoints you." He lifted the hammer. "Time to crack the shell."

*Low to moderate possibility of adaptation potential,* Whispy reported, excitement underlying the thought.

Trey and the other bounty hunters slowed until they were right behind James, their guns and wands at the ready.

James glanced over his shoulder and shook his head. "Let me handle this shit. You wanted a show, and I'll give you one."

Egorov licked his lips. "How about we make a deal, Brownstone? If I kill you, your guys let me go."

"Sure," James responded without hesitation.

Victoria, Ramon, and several of the bounty hunters frowned. Trey grinned.

"Oh?" Egorov replied. "You are really that confident?"

"I only need you alive," James replied. "That doesn't mean I can't hurt you." He held up his hand to the others. "Stay out of this shit."

Egorov threw back his head and laughed. "I don't even care if I die. If I take you with me, that's all I need. I'll be remembered forever."

"Talk less and kill me already," James ordered. "I'm kind of on the clock here, asshole."

Egorov sneered and charged, lifting the hammer. James swung his blade and sliced the man's hand off with one smooth motion. The hand and the hammer landed a few feet away with a soft thud.

The mobster howled in pain and fell to the ground, blood spurting from the stump. He rattled off something in Russian, gripping his wrist before looking up at James. "But my shield!"

James snorted. "Your second-rate shield wasn't gonna work against me." He marched over to the hammer and picked it up. "This shit might have, but fuck, no reason to be dumb about it." He placed the tool against the center of his armor, where his amulet peeked out.

*Drain it,* James commanded.

*Draining alternative power,* Whispy responded. *Analyzing underlying magic. Please note reduced efficacy of potential adaptation.*

*Just drain that shit.*

A few seconds later, the hammer crumbled into dust.

"No!" Egorov bellowed.

*Power drained. Minor adaptation achieved.* Whispy's annoyance radiated through their mental link.

*Huh, it was actually new?*

*Yes.*

*It's been a good four years since we last ran into that, even if we don't play all that often. I wonder how it would have worked,* he thought.

*Impossible to determine tactical effectiveness from indirect drain,* Whispy noted. *In next encounter, recommend direct engagement with weapon.*

James grunted. *I should maybe die just so you can be less bored?*

*That, and improved tactical efficiency.*

James nodded at the wounded mobster. "Probably should get that bleeding under control, Victoria. He can't squeal to the cops if he's dead, but we're not wasting a healing potion on this sonofabitch."

The witch chuckled and walked over to the mobster, her wand in hand.

James nodded to Trey, then the hallway. Both men exited while the witch tended James' victim.

"We've got total control," Trey explained. "The police are on their way."

James' helmet retracted, melting into the top of his armor. "Good. Now do you need any other favors, or can I get back on the road?"

Trey laughed and patted James' armored arm. "Nah. We're good. Thanks for the assist, big man."

James offered him a nod and looked back at Victoria. She'd sealed the wound, but hadn't bothered to try to reconnect the severed hand. He wasn't even sure if her healing magic was that good.

"It's fun to get a little exercise now and again," James admitted, gazing at the agency bounty hunters cuffing prisoners down the hallway. "But all the chasing people around shit gets old."

"No one's gonna complain if you want to un-retire, you know." Trey raised an eyebrow. "It's not like we bitch because bounties are too easy."

"My wife will, and probably my new kid would complain if I un-retired." James shook his head. "Nope. The occasional favor will have to be enough. I kicked enough ass before I retired. I've earned a break."

"Not saying you don't." Trey nodded. "And you're the man paying the bills. You know where to find us if you get bored playing with your barbeque." He pointed down the hallway. "We won't need you for the rest. If the cops bitch about Egorov, I'll handle it. You better get back on the road. It's like you said—you're supposed to be hitting barbeque, not bounties."

*Recommend additional tactical engagement,* Whispy suggested.

*Nope. Trey's right. It's time for more barbeque.*

*Please note that barbeque is of questionable tactical value.*

*I can't believe any symbiont of mine would believe that,* James sent. *You sure you're really Whispy Doom?*

*Emotional attachment doesn't increase the tactical value of sauced and grilled meat,* Whispy responded.

*Keep telling yourself that and I'll slap some sauce on you and eat you.*

James' wide grin made Trey eye him.

"What's up?" Trey asked.

"Nothing," James replied. "Just thinking about how important barbeque is."

Trey snickered. "Talk about a one-track mind."

# CHAPTER TEN

James stifled a yawn as his truck barreled down the 15, Vegas growing more distant with each passing minute. Despite all Whispy's modifications, including passive regeneration, James still needed to sleep. There was probably some fundamentally important biological truth underlying that reality, but James didn't really care. Sometimes it was nice just to rest, especially after a couple of days of handling bounties. He still had a few hours of driving that day, though.

"It's like I didn't even retire," James muttered to himself. "Taking down bounties, fighting power-armored mercs."

With plenty of hours of daylight left and a schedule to keep, James shrugged off the fatigue. His gaze cut to the phone on his console. He grabbed it and dialed, setting it to speaker.

The phone rang a few times.

"Hey, Dad, what's up?" Alison answered.

"Nothing. Just driving, and I'm bored," James admitted.

"You're not busy beating someone down, are you? I can call back."

Alison laughed. "You think I'd answer my phone in the middle of a fight?"

"I might if it were you calling." James grunted. "Especially if the other guy wasn't that tough."

"Good to know, but I'm pretty sure you don't generally keep your phone on you in the middle of a fight." Alison snickered. "Mom mentioned you left on your little road trip. I hope you're having good barbeque and a good time."

James checked his mirrors, but there weren't any other cars around. There might be a hidden Alliance ship for all he knew, but he figured it'd be another few decades before they mustered the courage to go after him again, especially since he'd taken down five Vax singlehandedly.

"I spent a couple of days in Vegas," James explained. "I was just supposed to stop by for some Jesse Rae's and to see Trey, but he dragged me into some shit with golfing wizards and Ultimate."

"Golfing wizards? Wait, Ultimate?" Alison sighed. "I've heard a little bit about it, but we're not seeing it up here yet. My law enforcement contacts haven't mentioned it showing up either. I suppose it was inevitable someone made something like that, as opposed to using artifacts to do it."

"I didn't mean to call and talk about drugs. Let's talk about something not related to work. I mean ass-kicking work. We can talk about barbeque if you want."

Alison sighed. "Well, there *is* something I want to talk about that doesn't have to do with work. It's personal."

"You know you can always talk to me." James' hands

tightened on the wheel. He always wanted his daughter to talk to him, but he was the first to admit he often struggled when Shay wasn't around to translate the subtlety of certain emotions for him.

"I know you...object to me moving in with Mason," Alison began, "but I—"

"No," James declared.

"No? Come on, Dad. That's not fair." Alison sucked in a breath and slowly blew it out. "And I wasn't asking for permission, just to be damned clear."

James grunted. "You're not understanding me."

"Then explain yourself," Alison snapped.

James frowned and took a few seconds to gather his thoughts. "I'm not saying no to Mason. I'm saying no to my complaints before. They were crap, and I thought I'd made that clear after Vancouver, but I guess I didn't. I'm not gonna pretend I wasn't pissed, and I didn't like the idea at first, and I'm not gonna lie about how much I bitched to your mom about it. If I hadn't gotten sidetracked by the pregnancy news, I probably would have driven up there to have another loud conversation with Mason."

"And now?" Alison asked softly.

"It's like I told him after the fight—I expect him to be a man, and be there for you." James shook his head, his over-protectiveness warring with other instincts. "The thing is, seeing him in action during that raid changed things for me. I know he'll have your back, not just when you're feeling upset, but when dark wizards are trying to kill you with some super-artifact jar. That's a good thing in a boyfriend."

Alison laughed. "I'm glad you've come around. Again, it

wasn't like I was asking for permission, but I'm still happy to hear all this. I want the men in my life to get along."

James glanced at the phone for a second before returning his attention to the road. "This thing with Mason seems a lot more real than anything you've had in a long time, not that you've always been that open about your love life."

"I suppose you can say that. We both know I had my issues because of Tanner. Maybe there would have been someone else with a real connection had I given them the chance, but you know, I've got Mason now, and he's understanding about everything in my life. I can't ask for much more."

"So when are you meeting his parents?" James asked.

"W-what?" Alison sputtered.

"His parents." James grunted. "He's met *your* parents. From what you told me, he's not an orphan or some shit like that, so he's got parents somewhere. Right?"

"Yes, he has parents." Wariness underlaid Alison's voice.

"And he doesn't hate their asses. Right?"

"Not really," Alison whispered. "He's had his disagreements with them, but he talks to them. They're not on bad terms or anything."

James nodded to himself. "Then don't you think you should meet them? If he's met your family, then it's only fair that you meet his."

"I'm not sure. It's a big step."

James chuckled. "I'm not saying you should start sending invites to your local Mafia dons, but if you're moving in together, you're at least heading that way. Don't you think you should meet his parents?"

Alison let out a long sigh. "I'll be honest, Dad. I don't know where this is going. I'm not saying I can't see marriage down the line, but I'm also not sure. I do love him, but every once in a while, I wonder if I'm seeing and feeling more than is there."

"He loves you, right? He's said it?"

"Yes," Alison murmured. "He said it first, way before I said it. He's always been up front in the feelings department."

"I'm far from an expert on this kind of thing, but it sounds like you're both looking in the same direction. You even have a practice kid with that Sonya there," James offered.

Sonya, a teenage witch who specialized in infomancy, a type of computer and systems magic, had ended up living with Alison after some of her employees and friends had tracked the girl down, thinking she was a dangerous enemy. The poor kid had been left by her father and abused by her mother because of her magic, but now she had a new chance at life.

Alison groaned. "'Practice kid?' Dad, don't go seeing babies everywhere just because you have one coming. I'm *so* not ready for a kid. You know, other than Sonya, and Tahir and Hana are doing all the heavy lifting with her anyway."

"I wasn't ready for a kid either, but I did okay, and you turned out great."

"It's not the same thing, Dad. My life is complicated right now."

James laughed. "You're seriously trying that line on me?"

"It's true," Alison replied, irritation in her voice. "Just because we solved Izzie's problem doesn't mean everything else has gone away. There's all the Drow stuff to worry about. I mean, not right now, but eventually."

James took a deep breath and slowly let it out, his gaze fixing on the horizon for a moment. "Time for a little life lesson, Alison."

"Why am I already terrified?"

James could almost hear her rolling her eyes.

"When I met you and your mom, my whole philosophy of life was about keeping shit simple."

"I know. You only said it, like, every other second. The only thing you talked about more was barbeque." Alison scoffed.

James grunted. "The point is, I know a little about things being complicated, but you know what else I learned from all that?"

"Blow up major international criminal rings *before* they send assassins after you?" Alison suggested.

"Nah. I learned that no matter how much you want to keep shit simple, it's always complicated. That's life. Even if I wasn't a bounty hunter and I had just been running my restaurant back then, I would have had other complicated shit to worry about. If you're waiting to take the next step because you want life to get less complicated, you'll be waiting until King Oriceran dies of old age. I don't know if either of us will live that long."

Alison fell silent for so long that James began to wonder if the line had gone dead.

"Thanks," she finally whispered. "You've given me a lot to think about, and you're right. I'm going to try to trust my feelings more. I'm not saying that means anything other than the move, but I'm glad I have your support."

"You've always had it, and you always will," James intoned. "You need any right now? If you've got Drow breathing down your neck, maybe they need a little visit from the man who took down Laena."

Alison chuckled. "Nope. Like I said, it's all under control for now. They might be pulling a few schemes, but this isn't like before. I don't think anyone's going to send crazed assassins or try to summon strange monsters to get at me."

"Just saying, I could change directions and head up to Seattle."

"No, seriously, it's fine, Dad. I'm fine, and you've seen my friends in action, and we didn't even have my entire team from the company. You should just relax and enjoy your barbeque." Alison let out a contented sigh. "A baby, huh? I'll admit I would kind of prefer a younger brother."

"A younger brother?" James replied. "Why?"

"I've got the big sister/little sister thing going on with Sonya, so it'd be nice to mix it up. What about you?"

James furrowed his brow. "Either is fine." He frowned. There had been a noticeable absence of one sensitive topic in the conversation. "You really sure everything else is all right?"

"Yes," Alison replied quietly. "If you're talking about what I think you're talking about, then, yeah. I'm dealing with it, and Mason and Hana and the others are helping me. Losing people is hard, but it's not like I haven't dealt with it before. In this case, though, I'm trying to make sure I'm living up to the sacrifice."

James scoffed. "Living up to it? You've been living up to it for years. No matter what happens, I want you to know how proud I am. Your sibling will have one hell of a sister to live up to."

"Ahh. Thanks, Dad."

"I'm gonna let you go for now. I'm sure you have better things to do than talk to me on the phone. I love you, and give me a call if you need anything."

"I love you, too. Talk to you soon."

James reached over to his phone to end the call.

*Hell, no matter what happens, at least I'm one for two when it comes to kids.*

# CHAPTER ELEVEN

James leaned back in his chair, a pile of clean ribs sitting on the plate in front of him as he finished up his meal at the Spitfire Smokehouse in Moab, Utah. This was the kind of experience he wanted, traveling the road and finding out-of-the-way barbeque joints and experiencing their flavor profiles, not taking on mercs in power armor and drug-enhanced wizards.

*Shay was right. I needed this shit. I just need to stop getting dragged into bounties.*

It was easy to find criminals to beat down, but finding quality barbeque could be a challenge. This wasn't his first barbeque road trip, but it'd been a few years since the last.

*Huh. And that shit* still *ended with me having to beat someone down. Well, at least I got it out of the way this time. I'm sure when I get to Denver, I won't have any problems at all.*

The restaurant's owner cleared his throat from behind the counter. "We don't get a lot of celebrities in here, let alone celebrities who know about barbeque. I'm almost afraid to ask, but how was everything?"

James nodded to the man. "It was great. I've got no complaints." He gestured at his plate.

The owner pulled out his phone with a nervous smile on his face. "I'm sure you get asked all the time, but could I get a picture with you? It might help business if people knew James Brownstone had eaten here."

James stood and headed over toward a wall that had a laminated menu hanging on it. "Sure."

The owner scurried over beside James and held out the phone for a selfie. He took a few pictures with a huge smile on his face. "Thank you, Mr. Brownstone. I appreciate it."

"No problem." James extended his hand. "And call me James."

The owner gave his hand a firm shake. "Sure thing, James."

"One thing before I head out." James turned and frowned out the window. "Does this town actually have a gas station?"

The other man nodded. "It's right before you get back on the highway. It's the only one we have left, but you can't miss it."

Before James headed toward the door, he fished out a few large bills and tossed them on the table. The man deserved a big tip for maintaining such quality in a small town.

The owner had no international fame, and no movies had been made about him or his daughter. He just had good-tasting food. In a sense, his barbeque was purer than James' or Nadina's.

James pushed out of the restaurant, thinking about the gas station. While LA didn't present much of a problem, he had found that with each passing year, it was growing harder to find gas stations. With electric vehicles now the strong majority, even his stubborn attachment to his decades-old truck couldn't stave off the inevitable. The reality was, at some point, he wouldn't be able to drive a gas-powered truck anymore. It might take ten or twenty more years, but the day was coming.

*Shit. What do I do? Put an electric engine in it? My F-350 wouldn't be the same with an electric, and even Alison's driving an electric Fiat. Trey traded in his truck when he had the kid.*

The future wasn't always kind to people and their tastes.

James grunted as he headed toward the parked Ford. There had to be some other possibility. Maybe he could split the difference for a while with some sort of hybrid system, or even track down a wizard to create some sort of ever-full gas can. There had to be something like that. What was the point of magic if it wouldn't help a man keep his beloved truck?

*I've repaired that thing so many times. I've put enough money into it that I could have bought several new trucks, but maybe even a machine has to die eventually.*

Sighing wearily, James threw open the door and climbed inside. It was time to fuel up and continue toward Denver. He would enjoy his truck while he could.

---

*I wish they would just come over and ask for the fucking auto-graph already,* James thought, shaking his head as he continued pumping gas.

Two men had been lingering against the wall of the closed convenience store. Apparently, no one needed any snacks in the early evening in the town.

The men murmured to each other as they took sips of their beer, occasionally spilling some on their torn jeans and their Atlantis and Doom t-shirts. Judging by the font, Atlantis and Doom was some sort of metal band, but James paid about as much attention to music as he did anything else non-barbeque or family-related, which was not at all. You couldn't eat music.

When James had driven up, they'd both glanced his way and fallen into hurried whispers, pointing at him a few times.

James had ignored them as he finished filling his tank. He put the nozzle back on its rest and replaced his gas cap.

The men shared a look before nodding to each other. They tossed their beer bottles into a nearby garbage can and walked toward James, their hands in their pockets.

"Can I help you?" James rumbled.

One of the men scratched his cheek. "That's a sweet-ass truck you got. An actual F-350, right? I've got an eye for classic trucks. My dad was a mechanic. Died fixing a Chevy, actually. Funny story." He grinned. "Well, it's kind of one of those 'you had to be there at the time' things."

James nodded slowly. "Yeah, sounds hilarious." He frowned.

Both men kept a hand in a pocket. Obvious tension tightened their necks and shoulders. The other man's eyes kept darting back and forth as if looking for something or something.

*Don't do anything stupid, idiots.*

"So, uh," the first man continued. He sighed. "I'm gonna have to ask you to hand over your keys."

James stared at him. "Say that again?"

The man pulled out a switchblade and pressed the button. The blade extended with a click. "Your keys, bro. I know some guys who will pay a shit-ton of cash for a classic truck in that good of condition. Nothing personal. You hand over the keys and your phone, and we don't have trouble. It's not that long of a walk to a place where you can call someone, but it'll be long enough that we can get the hell out of here."

The thug's friend pulled out his own switchblade, unease on his features.

James laughed. What kind of criminal tried to rob a large tattooed man in a big truck, armed with only a knife? For that matter, what kind of criminal tried to rob James Brownstone with a knife?

"Do you seriously not know who I am?" James frowned.

"You a cop?" the first thug asked, squinting.

"No, I'm not a cop," James growled.

The second thug's eyes widened and he slowly backed away. "No, no, no. It can't be. Oh, shit. This is bad. This is very bad."

His friend kept his attention on James as he spoke. "What? He some fucking MMA bitch or something? That don't make him immune to getting stabbed, especially if we both take him on."

"No, you dumbshit," his friend shouted. "That's James Brownstone."

"I thought he was dead or some shit." The first thug narrowed his eyes.

"I'm not dead, moron," James rumbled. "I just don't do many bounties anymore."

"You're not James Brownstone." The man shook his head. "This is bullshit. You're just some fucker who looks like him. What are the chances that James Brownstone would be in Moab?" He waved the knife. "And Brownstone has, like, magic armor and shit, so give me the keys or I start getting stabby, bro."

His friend tossed his knife on the ground and raised his hands. He slowly backed away. "I don't want any part of this. This is suicidal."

"You cowardly little bitch." The first thug spat on the ground. "When I sell this thing, you don't get shit, you hear me? Not shit, and I'm gonna tell everyone how you were such a pussy."

James raised his hand and gestured for the man to come at him. "Okay, let's get this over with. An asshole trying to take me down with a knife? I can't even be angry about this shit, it's so ridiculous. At least if it was a magic knife, it wouldn't be so bad."

"Just give up!" the other thug yelled. "He's gonna kick you through a window."

James shook his head. "Nope. I don't want to cause trouble for whoever owns this place."

The knife-wielding thug grinned. "Yeah, I thought so. You're not Brownstone. Make up whatever story you want, but I'm still taking your truck.

"No, I am." James cracked his knuckles. "I just want to make sure I'm delivering the pain only to whoever deserves it. I don't like to cause trouble for people who don't have it coming. So, fucking come on already before I die of old age, or turn your ass around and get the fuck out of here."

"You dumb piece of shit," the thug growled. "I'm gonna stick you but good, and you're gonna bleed out here."

"The last people who messed with my truck ended up dead," James snarled. "Want to join them?"

The thug thrust the knife, and James threw up his uncovered arm to block. He didn't want to ruin another shirt.

The blade penetrated deep into James' arm. Pain spiked from the wound, but it was easy to ignore. He'd felt far, far worse. Bonding with Whispy hurt more.

"See, you stupid bitch?" the thug yelled. "Now you've gone and done it."

James jerked his arm back and the thug's eyes widened as he lost his grip on the knife. He tripped, falling to the ground.

"The one and only chance you might have would be to surprise me and blow me into tiny little chunks," James rumbled. He reached up and yanked the blade out of his arm with a grunt before tossing the bloodied weapon over his shoulder. His wound throbbed. "Stabbing me with some toothpick?" He chuckled. "You couldn't win against Trey's grandma with that knife."

"Who the fuck is Trey? And why the fuck should I care about his grandma?"

"Trey's ten times the man you could ever hope to be." James reared back and slammed his foot into the man's chest.

The thug flew several yards before landing hard on his arm and screaming. He turned onto his back, his arm flopping. It was bent at an unnatural angle. "You broke my arm, you sonofabitch."

"Yeah, because you just stabbed me and wanted to steal my truck." James shrugged. "What are you bitching about? You're not even dead. You're doing a lot better than a lot of the idiots who come after me."

James' arm continued to throb, but the pain already had begun to dull. The wound should easily be healed by the time he arrived at his next stop. His basic level of regeneration, let alone what he could achieve with Whispy, was one of the reasons he'd stopped carrying healing potions years before.

The second thug pulled out his phone and dialed, staring at James the whole time. "Yeah, it's not an emergency. I mean, it kind of is. I want to turn myself in for armed robbery. Me and my friend just tried to mug a guy at the gas station. My friend tried to stab the guy, but he got fucked up. No, not the guy, my friend. Yeah. Yeah. I think it's James Brownstone. No. Yeah. No, seriously. Could you send someone to come and arrest us? Maybe send an ambulance for my friend? I'm pretty sure his arm is broken. No, we're not going anywhere. Okay." He stuck his phone in his pocket and shrugged.

James grunted and nodded to the man. "Smart move. Pick better friends."

The thug shrugged and sighed. "So, hey... This is gonna sound weird, but could I get an autograph before I go to jail?"

His friend lay on the ground, his moans growing louder.

"Sure," James rumbled. "Since you weren't a dipshit."

# CHAPTER TWELVE

James glanced around as the F-350 rolled down the streets of Denver. It was a nice day, and a lot of people were out walking.

He'd had no more trouble on the road between Moab, Utah and his final destination. After his late arrival, he'd checked in at his hotel, called his wife, taken a quick shower, and gone to sleep, hopeful he could get through another day without any more ass-kicking detours.

That morning, after a lot of hotel bacon and sausage, James had decided he wanted to go check out the exterior of Nadina's restaurant even though it wasn't opening until the next day. Originally, he had hoped to have more time after he arrived, but helping Trey and the agency out had eaten that time.

*No big deal. It's not like I had any big plans. I'm lucky I didn't end up having to fight a dragon or some shit when I crossed into Colorado.*

James turned right, and after half a mile, slowed his truck to a halt at a police barricade manned by a bored-looking officer. A decent crowd of people stood in the distance, filling the street. They were arranged in a half-circle around a man in front of a microphone stand and two speakers, surrounded by men holding white banners. They were speaking in front of an otherwise unassuming one-story building with a red-brick façade and a stylized yellow sign reading Spice and Spell.

*That's Nadina's place. Shit. Did they open already?*

James pulled his truck off to the side and parked, then retrieved his phone to check the invitation message. The date and time confirmed the grand opening was the following day, but maybe Nadina had arranged some sort of ceremony? She would know James wouldn't be interested in that kind of thing, so she might have not bothered to tell him to come early.

*Not that different from when I opened my place. All those reporters wanted to show up. I think they were disappointed no one attacked my restaurant.*

James hopped out and headed toward the crowd. Whoever was speaking was shouting and some in the crowd were shouting back, but he couldn't make out what they were saying at that distance. It didn't sound like a friendly exchange, though.

People could be very passionate about barbeque. It was hard to blame them. Everything great in life inspired passion.

The police officer at the barricade eyed James for a moment, then nodded to another cop standing closer to the restaurant. A small smile broke out on the second cop's face, and he jerked his head toward the crowd.

*What the fuck is going on? Maybe he knows I'm supposed to*

*be at the grand opening but doesn't realize I'm not supposed to be at whatever this thing is?*

James passed the barricade and walked toward the edge of the crowd. Many in the crowd automatically parted for him and allowed him easy passage toward the front. He wasn't sure if their reaction was because they recognized him or they were afraid of him.

He wasn't that far into the crowd when he was able to understand the speaker, and more importantly, he could read the text of the huge white banner held by two men.

*You've got to be kidding me.*

PROTECT OUR HUMAN VALUES. PROTECT OUR HUMAN LANDS. PROTECT OUR HUMAN CULTURE. JOIN THE HUMANITY DEFENSE LEAGUE.

Two other men held a smaller banner off to the side that said KEEP BARBEQUE HUMAN! ELVES SHOULD STICK TO ELF FOOD.

James scrubbed a hand over his face. Why couldn't the assholes just stay on the internet rather than screwing with a barbeque restaurant?

A half-dozen other HDL members in suits and white HDL armbands stood to either side of the speaker, solemn expressions on their face, their arms at their sides.

James grunted.

*Oh, those stupid fucks.*

The speaker, a bespectacled man with a pinched face, shook a fist in the air. "It's like I was just saying. Too many people concentrate on flashy magic. They believe that's the problem, but they're tragically missing the point." He snorted and shook his head. "We of the HDL aren't crazed terrorists like the New Veil. We don't want to hurt anyone, human or otherwise. We just want to protect humanity, and we realize things like magic aren't the problem." He pointed to his chest. "Humanity has its own magic, and we continue to develop that to better protect the planet against all non-human species that would seek to take it from us. Is that so wrong?"

A few people in the crowd exchanged nervous glances, but a few shouts of "No!" also emerged from the crowd.

*None of this shit has anything to do with barbeque.*

The HDL speaker pointed to the restaurant. "Spice and Spell. It sounds innocuous, doesn't it? You think it's just a restaurant?"

"It *is* just a restaurant, asshole!" someone shouted from the crowd. "Go back to where you came from. You people aren't even from Denver."

The man chuckled. "See? You understand. You have the right instincts. You want to protect your culture. So do I. I just understand that humanity has a cultural tapestry made up of unique threads of everything from barbeque to teppanyaki."

James moved closer. Two cops stood off to the side, frowning.

"I didn't want to be here today," muttered one of the cops. "I was supposed to be at my kid's Little League game. You sure all their permits are in order? Remember last month with those other protesters? They'd screwed the paperwork up."

The first cop nodded. "Yeah. There's nothing we can do unless they start something."

"He says they aren't terrorists, but there *are* HDL terrorists." The cop snorted. "I don't care what someone's politics are. I don't want any terrorist sympathizers in my town."

The cops' gazes drifted to James. The first cop leaned toward the second to whisper something, still looking at James, and the other nodded. Visible relief passed over their faces as both returned their focus to the speaker.

James chuckled.

The bespectacled man adjusted his tie. "And it's 'just a restaurant?' That's true, but that's what makes it even more pernicious." He flung his hand behind him. "Don't you see? Conquering a world is difficult. No, conquering a species is difficult, especially a species that has its own magic and advanced technology, including nuclear weapons." He gestured toward the crowd. "If the Oricerans had shown up and started destroying our cities like in *War of the Worlds* or *Magic Apocalypse,* we would have taken them out with ease. Also let me make it clear: the Oricerans aren't evil. We of the HDL don't believe they are boogeymen. We understand they are from a planet with many different species, but those species aren't human, even if they look like us." He laughed. "And I can understand why you're all puzzled. A beautiful woman wants to open a barbeque restaurant? Where's the harm, right?"

Waves of shouted agreement and irritation swept through the crowd.

"Just think of it as slow colonization under the guise of assimilation," the speaker continued. "They'll come, take what's ours, change it until it's theirs, and then claim it. It'll put us off-guard, make us think they're adapting to our ways, but they're actually taking over our culture, until the next thing we know, everything important in our world is run by Oricerans and humans are second-class citizens on their own planet. In a way, this restaurant is worse than a straightforward attack. At least an attack is honest."

James pushed forward. He'd had enough of this crap, and he hadn't driven all the way up from LA so a bunch of loud-mouthed idiots could interfere with his ability to taste some quality barbeque.

A hush fell over the crowd. The other HDL members narrowed their eyes.

The speaker stared at James for a few seconds, something approaching satisfaction on this face. "You're James Brownstone, right?"

"Yeah," James rumbled.

"You're a bounty hunter who has fought many dangerous non-human creatures." The speaker gave him a warm smile. "I have to personally thank you. You and your men saved a cousin of mine from a Council attack. Amusement park trip from hell. You, better than anyone, understand that Oricerans can be dangerous even if they look us."

"Sure," James responded. "I guess that's true."

Gasps erupted from the crowd. James looked their way. There were no obvious Oricerans present. That was probably for the best. The HDL might have tried to start something if there were.

James turned back toward the speaker. "But big fucking deal. Plenty of humans are dangerous too, and I've taken out way more of them than Oricerans. Being a bounty hunter is about dangerous assholes, not just dangerous Oriceran assholes."

The speaker chuckled nervously, his expression turning

uncertain. "Sure, but you're also famous as a barbeque lover. I'm sure you could give us all insight into how this elf woman has perverted something so human at its core. Cooking is the soul of a culture, and an outsider, a non-human, can never capture that. At best, it'll be a hollow imitation, a mockery."

James reached up and scratched his cheek, then took a deep breath and shook his head. "Cooking is the soul of the culture. I agree with that."

The speaker nodded. "Right? There you have it, my friends. Even James Brownst—"

"I'm not done talking," James rumbled, his voice coming out close to a growl.

"Of course. Feel free to continue."

James pointed at the HDL speaker. "You're no pitmaster, and you and your friends are a bunch of dipshits who don't know anything about me, and certainly don't know shit about the true soul of barbeque." He raised his voice until it was a booming shout. "You're all a bunch of weak-ass bitches with weak-ass whiny signs who probably couldn't tell North Carolina from Texas-style if you had a fucking wand pointed at your head."

Silence choked the area. The HDL speaker stared at James, his eyes bulging.

"If you want to show Nadina up when it comes to barbeque," James shouted, "you should beat her in a competition, not by protesting."

The HDL speaker sucked in a breath through gritted teeth. "This isn't about barbeque," he replied. "I don't even like barbeque. This is about protecting what is human. Can't you understand that?"

James scoffed and pointed up the street away from the crowd. "You don't like barbeque? Then get the fuck out of here. This is a barbeque restaurant, not fucking Congress."

The other man rubbed his temples, exasperation spreading over his face. "This doesn't have anything to do with you, Mr. Brownstone. You might use magic armor, but you're still human. Why are you sticking up for an elf?"

*Yeah, if anything, Nadina's probably closer to a human than I am, but good thing the average dipshit still thinks Whispy is just magic armor.*

James snorted. "And I thought everyone knew everything about me. My daughter's a half-elf, you stupid motherfucker, but that doesn't even matter."

The HDL speaker glared at James. "And why is that?"

"Because I might defend the Devil if he opened a nice barbeque joint."

A few people in the crowd laughed.

James curled a hand into a fist and raised it. "So get the fuck out of here, and I better not see your ugly-ass faces or signs back here."

"We have a legal right to be here," the speaker shouted.

James shrugged. "I have a right to spout off too. That's what's so great about America, asshole. If you want me out of here, then drag my ass out." He offered them a hungry grin. "I'd love to see you try."

The HDL members exchanged glances before the speaker grabbed the microphone stand and nodded toward the rest of their equipment. A couple other men picked up the speakers and fell in behind the retreating HDL members.

A few people in the crowd clapped, but most looked confused.

The two closest police officers made their way over to James.

"Thanks, Mr. Brownstone," one of them offered. "I hate those pricks, but there's nothing we can do."

"No reason to thank me." James shrugged. "I was just defending barbeque."

CHAPTER THIRTEEN

The next day, James again walked down the street toward Nadina's restaurant. Though no police barricades or cars blocked the street, he wasn't able to find any parking close to the building.

A line of private security in black uniforms stood in front of Spice and Spell. A pack of reporters, cameramen, and hovering camera drones lingered in the area, but no protesters—or if they were protesters, they were extremely well-dressed. He spotted a single police car parked down the block with no officers inside. All the tension from the previous day was gone.

A small crowd of people in tuxedos and cocktail dresses lingered near the entrance, chatting quietly as they filtered in and out of the packed restaurant.

*Who the hell wears a tuxedo to a barbeque place? Are all of Nadina's openings like this? Good thing I have avoided them so far.* James frowned and looked down at his jeans and t-shirt. He shook his head. There had been far fewer reporters when his restaurant opened, which made it a far less annoying event, but his antipathy for people sticking cameras in his face was well known.

As if sensing his discomfort, a dark-haired reporter spun and all but charged him, a camera drone keeping station a few yards behind and above him. Everybody might know what he didn't like, but that didn't mean they were always smart about it.

The reporter smiled. "Now, this is unusual. James Brownstone. I knew you were invited, but you never come to things like this. A once-in-a-lifetime event!"

James grunted. "I don't think me showing up at a barbeque place is all that weird. I like barbeque. That's not a secret. Who the hell are you, anyway?""

"I'm Kyle Killoughby. I'm with the Food Fusion channel." The reporter extended his microphone. "Would you be willing to answer a few questions for our viewers?"

A few other hungry reporters glanced his way. They looked so desperate to pounce on him that James was surprised they didn't lick their lips and start drooling.

Alison had suggested to him that her recent experiences proved cultivating a good media image with a few select organizations could be helpful. That might be true, but he didn't have the patience for it. He didn't need the media, and they didn't care about him, other than how he could help them. Accordingly, politeness was something he didn't bother with when it came to reporters.

"Questions?" James muttered. "Depends on the questions."

"Would you care to comment on reports that you dispersed an angry anti-Oriceran mob that was about to set fire to the restaurant?" Kyle asked. "Initial reports suggest you almost attacked an HDL protest."

"That's kind of overblown. We just had a loud discussion."

The reporter raised an incredulous eyebrow. "'A loud discussion?' That's what you're calling it?"

"The cops were there. Ask them." James snorted. "Hey, we live?"

*I know one way to end this shit.*

Kyle bobbed his head. "Yes, Mr. Brownstone. We're being streamed live."

James grinned. "Then I'll make it clear to your audience. I didn't do much. All I did was run off some stupid mother-fuckers who don't understand barbeque. Those dipshits were more concerned about something other than the food, which is the only thing anyone should care about at a motherfucking restaurant." With a grunt, he pushed past the blinking reporter.

"There you have it," Kyle stammered. "James Brown-stone offering colorful commentary on local anti-Oriceran protests at Nadina's new restaurant."

James glared at the other reporters, and they all found somewhere else to look, all the eagerness from before left their faces. The security guards glanced his way, but no one challenged him or asked him for an invitation.

Sometimes fame had its advantages. The HDL show-down the day before had left him annoyed, and today he just wanted to sit down and dig into some good barbeque.

James stepped inside and waited at the podium. There was no one there, which was unsurprising given how busy everything was.

Unlike the modest and small dining room at James' place, Nadina's restaurant was huge. Dark tables filled the cavernous dining room. A huge bar ruled the center, multiple bartenders smiling as they set bottles and glasses in front of customers. Dark-clad waiters and waitresses flitted from table to table, many holding massive silver trays filled with not only with the expected foods such as ribs and brisket, but also sauced and grilled vegetables.

*All these places, and she doesn't even use magic for decoration. Would people accept her if she did? Most of the crowd didn't seem like it was on the HDL's side, but maybe people in Denver really like fancy restaurants, even if they are barbeque.*

The chaotic din of excited chatter filled the air. No one looked James' way. A small number of reporters with cameramen wandered the dining room, but most people appeared to be happy customers, including a few other pitmasters James recognized from the competition scene.

The rest of the crowd, judging by their too-perfect faces, bodies, and smiles, were celebrities, actors, and musicians. He recognized Jericho Cartwright, a pretty-boy action star, if only because he'd watched one of the man's movies after Alison had mentioned meeting him and being unimpressed. The movie had sucked, but James didn't care for most movies, so he might be judging it too harshly.

James surveyed the room for a long moment before grunting. Nadina was conspicuously absent from the crowd.

*She must be in the back, supervising the food.*

A smiling redhead stepped out of a back door and was hurrying toward the podium when she spotted James. "I'm sorry for the wait, Mr. Brownstone. We've been expecting you."

James shrugged. "Doesn't look like there is anywhere for me to sit anyway. I'll just wait."

The woman shook her head, her smile never leaving her face. "We have a table reserved for you." She gestured into the dining room after pulling a menu off the podium. "If you would follow me?"

James chuckled as the woman led him through the crowded dining room. Everyone looked ridiculous, trying to eat barbeque in their tuxedoes and expensive dresses. He winced as he saw someone cut into a slab of sauced tofu, part of Nadina's well-promoted "vegetarian" barbeque. He might not be a purist, but he felt that barbeque should, by definition, include meat.

*Well, not everything she does has to be good, and maybe if the vegetarians are around enough people eating normal barbeque, they'll switch sides, or at least they'll try real barbeque when they're in a barbeque place.*

The woman led James around a corner to an empty table he hadn't been able to see. A few people glanced his way before returning to their meals and conversation.

James took a seat and accepted a menu from the smiling woman.

"Your server will be with you in a moment," she explained before retreating toward the front of the restaurant.

James flipped open the menu. It presented a complicated puzzle of meat and sauce choices, more a book than a simple guide to available meals. It was the antithesis of the KISS philosophy, but he wasn't surprised. Many of Nadina's places had complicated menus, and although there were some mainstays on her menu, every restaurant was unique in its own way, from décor to food choices

*Maybe she* does *use magic if she's making all of this stuff. Shit, just ingredient-sourcing has to be a pain in the ass.*

The initial section of the Spice and Spell's menu focused on protein selection, followed by sauces and then sides. Mainstays like chicken, pork, and beef were available, along with more exotic choices including buffalo and emu, and even one of the few Oriceran meats approved for wide distribution, aquaboar. He hadn't seen it at any of Nadina's other places he'd eaten at.

James had tried it once and hadn't been overly impressed, more because of the odd tangy aftertaste than the high price. He figured most barbeque fans preferred good old-fashioned pig, but since Nadina's restaurants varied in their target audiences, it wasn't a bad move to include it.

He'd visited one of her places in Texas long after the opening. It served almost entirely standard Texas barbeque with a little Carolina on the side, even if it still managed to have an overly complicated menu. The Spice and Spell seemed to be trying to hit a different crowd.

*Is there really a bunch of rich hipsters interested in barbeque? I shouldn't complain. The more people who like barbeque, the better.*

Nadina's restaurants benefited from their more lenient government importation stances on Oriceran spices compared to Oriceran meats, but the sauce notes in the menu only listed the Earth ingredients, with a few cutesy notes such as "enhanced by a delicious touch from Nadina's homeland."

James grunted. Details determined everything in food. It was hard to evaluate things before tasting it without that information.

The chicken, pork, and beef were also offered in different versions, including live-animal derived, synthetic, and vegetarian-simulated. He gritted his teeth at the final option.

Simulated meat was just wrong. It was a lie. The thought made his stomach tighten. Plants shouldn't pretend to be meat or vice-versa, no matter how things were on Oriceran.

*Fuck, the way things are going, magic's gonna produce some weird shit even if Nadina stays away from using it in her recipes. I should ask a vegetarian sometime: if a plant's moving around on its own and eating things, does that make it not okay to eat?*

Given some of the things he'd seen from Zoe over the years, James wasn't so sure there was such a clean line between plant and animal on Oriceran.

James sighed and returned his attention to the menu, pondering magic as applied to barbeque.

Decades after the return of magic, the FDA was still grappling with the implications, including long-term studies of the safety and health impacts of magically-modified organisms. The federal government had punted by restricting a number of Oriceran imports and sticking warning labels on most products. *Caveat emptor* if someone ended up growing a new arm after eating enchanted cheese.

James' home state, as was its tendency, overreacted by

putting even more extreme warnings on everything. The way California made it sound, everyone was going to drop dead from cancer caused by a magical casting a light-orb spell ten miles away. While it wasn't as if being dubious of magic was unreasonable, when everything had a warning label on it, such things became pointless.

In James' case, he didn't care. Even if his current life-style was, most weeks, far less dangerous than it had been years ago, he knew one important fact. An enchanted piece of meat wasn't going to be the thing that took him out, and if he had to choose a way to die, death by barbeque was as good an option as any.

A waiter made his way from another table, tablet in hand. "Can I get you something to drink, sir?"

"Give me your best Irish Stout," James rumbled. "You have that, right?"

He didn't want to drink wine with his barbeque.

"Yes, sir." The waiter tapped in the order. "Are you ready to order? Please be aware, Mr. Brownstone, that everything is on the house for you, courtesy of Nadina."

James shrugged. "Not like I can't pay, but whatever. Do you have some sort of sampler tray? I kind of want to taste everything." He grimaced. "Everything from an actual animal. No synthetic meat. No fake meat. I don't care how much it allegedly tastes like real meat. If it didn't come from something with legs to begin with, I don't want it."

"Yes, sir." The waiter chuckled. "Very good, sir. Nadina anticipated you'd request something like that. I'll put in your order right away and go get your stout."

"Thanks. I appreciate it."

The waiter walked off, his crisp shirt, pants, and tie

incongruous amid the glories of barbeque as far as James was concerned.

A woman in a little black dress a few tables away was actually eating her ribs with a fork and knife. She might as well have been spitting in church.

James shook his head in disgust before smirking at the fact that most people were wearing black leather bibs. He only had paper ones at his restaurant.

The other Nadina restaurants he'd tried had varied. Some had cloth bibs, others paper, but he hadn't seen leather before.

*Does that mean they're cleaning those things here? That's gonna get obnoxious.*

Every once in a while, someone looked James' way, but most people didn't seem to take particular note of him. He was just another man in a room filled with celebrities. One balding man working on ribs with the delicacy of someone performing brain surgery even gave him a disgusted look as if surprised Nadina would allow some random man in jeans to attend the opening of her high-end eatery.

James relaxed into his seat. He wouldn't have to worry about strange meat, and the HDL wasn't daring to show their faces. His barbeque road trip wouldn't be defined by him going after mutant drug-enhanced wizards, but by the glories of sauces and grilled meats.

The waitstaff seemed competent. No reporters were messing with him, and no one was flooding over to harass him about autographs. He might not like everything on Nadina's menu, but he intended to spend the next hour stuffing himself with barbeque both as a customer and a competitor.

*Fancy barbeque might not be my thing, but it's not like it hurts anyone. I'm just going to enjoy my meat.*

A grin broke out on his face. Shay only tolerated barbeque. Alison liked it, but she'd fallen for the dark side of sushi, loving a type of food that involved animals without legs. However, his new kid would be his to mold from the beginning. As soon as the kid had teeth, he or she was getting barbeque. His child would grow up to love barbeque as much as James.

*I'll have him working the grill on a stool if I have to.*

---

James licked sauce off his fingers, his brow furrowed in concentration. He had just finished downing three pulled pork sandwiches. According to the waiter, they were supposed to be Piedmont style, which would make them a North Carolina style variant. The tang of the apple cider vinegar was there, along with notes of ketchup and a nice balanced heat from red pepper flakes. That didn't bother him. He needed it. Expected it, really, given the style. In addition, salt and sugar were present.

The problem was what else was there. There was some other subtle flavor in the sauce, a faint aromatic note he couldn't identify. It took him off-guard, and his quick devouring of the sandwiches was more his desperate attempt to identify the ingredient than hunger.

*I don't know what it is. That means it has to be something I've not had, or something I've had but haven't identified. Some Oriceran spice, maybe? I don't remember eating anything like this at any of Nadina's other places.*

While James didn't object to Oriceran spices, he had no interest in using them himself, which meant his experience with them was limited. He'd faced off with a few other pitmasters using them, including Nadina, sometimes winning and sometimes losing. Those results suggested they had their value but weren't inherently superior to Earth spices.

"How is everything?" a soft female voice asked from behind him. "I see you've tried ribs with several different sauces, several different types of sandwiches, and many different types of meats. Hmm. All live-sourced meat, though."

"Some's good," James admitted without looking behind him. "Some of it is very good. The pork is great. Most of these sauces are great. Not gonna say she nailed the Tennessee, though. It's maybe even a straight-up miss."

"Oh?"

"The flavor was a little weak, but the standard Texas and Kansas City are great. Beef and chicken are decent, but not at the level of her pork work. Not gonna say I love all these other weird-ass meats, but the KC-style emu was tastier than I thought. I'm not going to add it to my menu anytime soon, though." He grunted. "I ended up deciding to give the synthetic meat a try, but it's always the same."

"The same?" the woman asked, sounding amused.

"I know they say you're not supposed to be able to tell the difference." James shook his head. "But I can always tell. I guarantee, if you put a blindfold on me, I could tell."

"Interesting. Have you tried any of the vegetarian options?"

"Hell, no." James picked up a half-eaten rib as if he

could ward off the Vengeful Spirit of Vegetarianism. "Barbeque is about meat. Synthetic meat might not grow on an animal, but at least it's meat." His nostrils flared. "So, overall, all the pure meat options are good to great, nice sauce work, good bark technique, good temperature control. Are there some individual styles I didn't like? Yeah, sure. Occasionally she does something with a spice that doesn't work for me, but I'm sure these rich people from Denver will eat it up. The great thing about barbeque is that different styles work for different people."

The woman laughed softly. "You're consistently honest, James."

He frowned and turned around. He'd been assuming he was talking to a waitress.

Nadina stood there, smiling.

CHAPTER FOURTEEN

Nadina wore an emerald-green chef's uniform, the name of her restaurant embroidered in script above her pocket. Her blond hair had been woven into a series of intricate braids that might have needed spells to maintain, a few of the braids framing her pointed ears. She folded her arms, her soft lips curled up in a slight smile, no hint of anger in her eyes. The smooth-skinned woman might be mistaken for being in her twenties if she were human, but she was over a century old.

Despite a few stains on the uniform that proved Nadina had been cooking that night, it was hard to ignore the makeup, the bright lipstick, and the hairstyle. The woman projected glamour and beauty, but her current image more a celebrity chef ideal compared to her humbler initial appearance on *Barbeque Wars* years prior.

*Who would have thought she would come this far?*

James might have been annoyed and suspecting she was coasting more on style than skill if he hadn't tasted her food. He knew that she could grill, even if she pushed the occasional eggplant abomination as an alternative. It was just hard for him to relate to *wanting* to be in the public eye instead of hiding in the kitchen.

*I bet no assholes come into her place to try to get punched.*

James grunted as he processed the thought. She might not have that, but he had never had to deal with protestors outside his restaurant.

"My wife's always telling me I need to be careful what I say," James offered. "And here I am shitting on some of your food. It doesn't make any difference that I didn't know it was you."

Nadina laughed softly and took a seat across from James. "Honesty isn't a trait I dislike. People can lie, but food never does, and deluding myself about what I cook won't help me."

"Even when I'm bitching about how much I hate certain things?" James shrugged before taking a bite of another rib. No reason to dwell on the food he didn't like when there was plenty there he did.

A reporter's drone camera closed for a quick picture, retreating when James swept the room with a glare.

"Yes, even then. It's not as if you didn't just get done singing the praises of many of the things I've been serving tonight. No one will like everything, and I appreciate what a carnivore you are." Nadina folded her hands in front of her. "It's a matter of perspective for me."

"Perspective?"

Nadina nodded. "Yes. I've had a blessed career. When I started on *Barbeque Wars*, a lot of people believed I wouldn't make it. A lot of people mocked me for even daring to think I could cook something they felt represented the soul of America's regions."

"Yeah, but you proved them wrong." James had already admitted to her in the past that he'd had similar thoughts when he'd first heard about her, but once she had started winning, they'd disappeared. He respected the judges on the show and had no reason to question their decisions.

"I proved those doubters wrong, and many turned into supporters, but not all did." Nadina's smile wavered. "Some decided mockery wasn't enough. The mockery turned into death threats."

James' jaw tightened. "Yeah."

Even if he'd heard it before, it didn't make it any more comfortable. Criminals coming after him when he was a bounty hunter possessed a certain basic logic. Threatening someone for cooking good food passed into the absurd.

Nadina sighed. "You know what the real tragedy is?"

James shook his head.

"So many people thought I didn't understand what barbeque meant." Nadina stared at the tray of ribs. "But I understood from the beginning."

*Yeah. I doubt it'd make her feel any better if I told her the HDL protesters think she understands that well enough that she's part of a purposeful plot against the planet.*

The more James thought about it, the stupider it sounded. He loved barbeque probably more than anyone on Earth, and he doubted Oricerans would ever conceive of undermining the country or planet by pushing an elf as a pitmaster celebrity.

Oriceran chefs in other culinary areas hadn't received nearly as much attention or pushback. Apparently, the fiendish plot to undermine humanity wouldn't involve Oricerans becoming the best at making Beef Wellington or risotto at Michelin-star restaurants.

*Huh. Maybe this is proof people give more of a shit about barbeque than they do fancy cooking.*

"I've always known what food means to people," Nadina explained quietly, with a wistful look. "It's not so different on Oriceran, regardless of species, and I think that was why I became so obsessed with barbeque. It spoke to my soul, so I wanted to share my soul with the rest of the country and this world. It's the best gift I could give them to pay them back for the joy I've experienced since coming to Earth." She unfolded her hands and gestured to a tray of brisket. "But I'm also not a child, and I knew that walking the path originally, let alone continuing to do it in a high-profile way, meant a lot of people were going to criticize me for various reasons. I accepted that it would harden the hatred of certain people, even as I convinced others of my sincerity."

James nodded. "That's true. I don't think a lot about how no one gives a crap if someone who looks like me opens a barbeque restaurant."

"Anger and hatred aren't new." Nadina furrowed her brow. "Many people have this incorrect conception of Oriceran as a place of peace, but it's a tenuous peace that was born of blood and fire.

"You don't have to convince me. The few times I've gone to Oriceran, it's been to kick someone's ass."

"So I've heard." Nadina sighed. "I'm not saying any of this to complain." She gestured around the packed dining room. "Being able to share food with people means I'm sharing love. I'm bringing our worlds together in a special and delicious way. I hope that in some small way, that means the two worlds have far less of a chance of going through something like what happened to my planet, even if that's naïve."

James shrugged. "Probably doing more than me beating people up."

Nadina chuckled. "Probably. Anyway, all I've ever wanted was for people to give me a chance. If they don't like what I offer them, that's fine. That's their right, but I want them to try." She nodded toward the mostly-consumed tray of ribs. "And that's what you've always offered, James. I can't be angry just because you don't love everything I make. Your honesty comes from you at least trying. You've never dismissed my food either in private or publicly because of my background or my species, and that honesty is pure and refreshing in its own blunt way."

James chuckled. "I'll have to use that line on my wife and daughter the next time they bitch about me being an asshole."

"Feel free." Nadina let out a contented sigh. "I also knew you wouldn't like a lot of this rather extreme upscale fusion menu. You've always been a more old-school pitmaster, and there's nothing wrong with that, but I'll always appreciate how you've spoken up for me."

"Those HDL assholes were annoying. It's no big deal. Loudmouths. I knew if I said something, they would scurry off."

Nadina shook her head. "I don't just mean them. I mean in the past. While I might have a lot of unusual fame and influence as the first elf to really make it big in barbeque, you're James Brownstone, the Granite Ghost, the famous class-six bounty hunter." She gave him an appraising look. "I might be able to do magic, but I couldn't defeat the kind of enemies you have. You were famous from the moment you started participating in competitions."

"I'm retired now," James offered. "Being a bounty hunter doesn't mean much."

"You're retired? What about Chile?" Nadina smirked.

James averted his eyes. "I just kind of stumbled into that."

*Mostly. I've just kind of stumbled into a lot of shit these last few years. I can't help it if people are idiots.*

"I see." Nadina looked like she was trying hard to not burst out laughing. "My point is that you have more influence in our community than a lot of people, and if you'd spent a lot of time talking trash about me, it would have hurt my career and community acceptance. You could have sunk my career. You were already participating in competitions before your retirement. I remember the first time I heard about PFW."

James scoffed. "It always comes down to the food for me. Nothing else. Some Harriken asshole could enter a competition, and I'd still judge him fairly before kicking his ass."

Nadina snickered. "Oh, I believe you. I also remember what you said to that one judge at Pork Days at Texas A&M. When was that? I think it was five years ago now." She laughed and leaned forward to whisper, "I remember the exact look on that judge's face when you told him that he was 'a dumb motherfucker who should stick to eating eggplant steaks because he obviously had no idea what good barbeque was.'" She shook her head. "It's hard for me not to giggle every time I think about it. I don't think anyone had even spoken to that man like that in his entire life."

James frowned. "Wait, how do you know about that? You weren't in the room." He glanced around to make sure there were no reporters nearby.

"A friend told me about it." Nadina paused for a moment to offer a smile and a wave to a departing guest. "I've thought about thanking you for that for years at one of my openings, but you've been avoiding them. I wanted it to be special, and here we are five years later."

"I don't like…" James nodded to a reporter across the room, "…this kind of thing. That's why I don't like openings. I hated the circus when my place opened, and it wasn't nearly this bad."

"I understand," Nadina replied. "And let me be clear: I've never been offended by you turning me down. Honestly, at first, I wondered if you had something against me because I was a Light Elf, even though you respected my food."

James frowned. "My daughter's a half-elf. Everyone seems to forget that. Her looking human doesn't change that. It'd be pretty stupid for me to have something against elves."

Nadina nodded. "I haven't forgotten that, but that's one of the reasons I also wondered."

"Huh?"

"It's not like the Drow and Light Elves always get along." Nadina shrugged.

James grunted. "Oh. That makes sense."

"After dealing with you long enough, I realized your gruff nature is very much you and not a show. If I had to live in a country filled with honest but gruff men like you, I'd gladly do it." Her gaze flicked to Jericho Cartwright. "Whatever else you are, you're honest, unlike a lot of the celebrities I'm around. That said, I'll never lie and say I don't like the fame. It's fun. I've always liked being the center of attention, but I also like making other people happy. This career is a good way to do both. Win-win."

"I like people enjoying my food." James reached for another rib. "But I'm not sure if I really care if they're happy. I want them to have good barbeque." He turned his head, frowning slightly at a security guard passing the window. "Lots of security tonight. I expected some, but maybe not this many. You were really that worried about the HDL coming back?"

"It's complicated." Nadina sighed and raised her hand. "Would you mind if I made our conversation a little more private?"

James shook his head. "Go ahead."

A few quick movements of Nadina's hand followed. She opened her mouth, and a layered melody poured out—her native tongue. The air around the table shimmered for a second.

"It's a silence spell," Nadina explained, lowering her hands. "I'm sure the reporters will be trying to read our lips on their recordings later, but if I do anything else, it'll only make our discussion stand out more. It'll be the same if I disappear with you into the back. I've learned as a famous woman that sometimes the best place to hide is in front of everyone."

"I'm fine with not hiding." James bit off a chunk from his rib. Maybe if he looked casual, no one would pay extra attention. "So the security is more than you usually need?"

Nadina offered a shallow nod, disappointment creeping onto her face. "I'm used to death threats. I get them constantly, but there has been an uptick in the last few weeks. The FBI even contacted me to say that though they couldn't go into details, they did want to make me aware of the 'terrorist chatter' concerning me."

"HDL?"

Nadina nodded. "One of the splinter factions that is more violent."

"Terrorists are going to blow up a barbeque joint?" Even verbalizing the question offended James on just about every level possible. His put his rib down and curled both hands into fists.

Nadina shook her head. "The threat was against me specifically. I thought about canceling the opening, but if I do, they win. Even the FBI told me they didn't believe the HDL would target the restaurant while there were humans inside. They might be full of hatred, but they aren't as bad as New Veil."

James grunted. "Are there are any FBI agents around? Undercover?"

"No. They said they would send agents when they had a specific and credible threat." Nadina sighed. "They just wanted me to be aware in general, so they're worried enough to pass along the warning but not any personnel. The local police have said their hands are tied unless they have a specific and credible threat as well. Unfortunately, with the background level of threats I receive, they are concerned it's not a good use of their resources." She shook her head. "It's almost ridiculous when you think about it. Someone wants to kill me for cooking."

James frowned. "You have a head of security, right? I know you have bodyguards, but I never paid much attention to that kind of thing at competitions or when I was visiting one of your places."

"It's not like I have a huge team normally, but I do have somebody who coordinates that for me, yes. I've gone through a few, but the man who works for me now has worked for me for a year."

"Have him pass along the information the FBI sent you. I want to check if they have a bounty."

Nadina's eyebrows lifted. "Does that mean you're getting involved?"

"This isn't about bounties, it's about barbeque. But I don't want to reinforce bad habits, so I want to make sure there is at least some money involved." James picked up his stout and took a sip. "I'm not some do-gooder. I'm just a bounty hunter who likes barbeque, so I can't promise anything, but at the least, I can look into it."

Nadina's face brightened. "Then I thank you on behalf of myself and the world of barbeque. I'll introduce you to my chief of security later tonight. I don't want to provide too much fodder for the reporters. I need them and they need me, but I also know they'd love to spread stories about me, given the chance."

"Fine."

*So much for my relaxing road trip. Those assholes should have gone after a seafood place instead.*

CHAPTER FIFTEEN

Spending hours lounging around drinking beer and eating barbeque while waiting for people and the media to filter out of the restaurant wasn't a very painful challenge for James. The only annoying part was the occasional reporter wandering over for a quote or a question. He responded with a stock answer praising the spareribs, and they quickly lost interest. It wasn't like he had a reputation for deep insight or witty remarks.

It was one time James didn't mind being underestimated.

Nadina circulated throughout the night, the few minutes she had spent with James earlier not seeming any more special to observers than the time she spent with some of the other pitmasters and celebrities.

Time whittled away the crowd, the packed room becoming a crowded room, and finally a mostly empty room.

When almost all the media had abandoned the event,

Nadina approached James. "Why don't you join me in the back office, James? I've got a few things to show you."

They slipped around the corner to a door leading into the back. The hall led off in two directions: to the bright kitchen at one end, the layered scents of the night's meals leaving a trail anyone could follow, and a series of closed doors down the other path in the austere white hallway.

Nadina led James into a small, mostly unadorned office with a glass desk and a single tablet. A few cabinets rested against the wall, and a black leather loveseat was a more comfortable place to talk. A framed picture of the elf woman smiling as she was declared the winner of *Barbeque Wars* hung on the wall.

James had seen it before. She had one in each of her restaurants, a reminder of where her career had started.

*All that humility talk isn't total bullshit.*

Nadina nodded to the sofa as she pulled out her phone and tapped in a quick message. "My security chief Cyrus will be here in a moment. Thank you for agreeing to help."

"I'm not guaranteeing anything." James plopped down on the couch. It was comfortable, with the right balance of give and push.

*Why can't I get my couch at home to be like this?*

"Of course. I understand. It's a relief, though, to think a man of your skills might be helping. I have nothing but the highest praise for Cyrus' work, but let's be frank, James— you might be a famous pitmaster, but you're a legendary bounty hunter."

James shrugged.

Nadina sat behind the desk, her face lined with weariness. "It's strange how six months of preparation goes into one night. I've done this enough times you think it would be easy, but it's always so stressful, even when I'm not worried about death threats."

"I think I'll stick with one place for now," James replied.

"It's a lot less stress." Nadina smiled. "I wish I could be more like you."

"How so?"

"Satisfied with one place." Nadina leaned her head against her chair. "I never really tried, you know, but I also kind of knew I wouldn't be."

"We all have our different ways of appreciating barbeque," James replied.

A dark-haired, broad-shouldered man in a dark-blue suit entered. He scowled after glancing at the two pitmasters.

Nadina nodded toward the door. "Shut the door, please, Cyrus."

The man complied and stared at James. "I haven't had the pleasure."

Nadina smiled. "Cyrus MacNamara, James Brownstone."

The security chief offered a thin smile. "Of course, I know who he is. Everyone knows who he is."

James grunted, thinking back to the punks in Utah. "You'd be surprised. Normally I don't give a shit, but every once in a while it becomes a problem."

"I can't imagine a man like you has a lot of problems he can't handle."

"That's one way of putting it."

Nadina took a deep breath. "James has generously offered to at least look into our potential security problem." She held up a hand. "He's not guaranteeing anything, though."

Cyrus folded his arms, the scowl returning. "May I speak freely?"

Nadina nodded. "You know I always prefer that you do."

Cyrus turned toward James. "We don't need a loose-cannon retired bounty hunter's help. No offense, Brown-stone, but bodies tend to pile up whenever you're around, and I get paid to make sure Nadina stays alive and her restaurants undamaged."

James snorted. "Yeah, bodies pile up, of people who have it coming. You got any proof I've killed an innocent person? And if I damage anything, I pay for it."

Cyrus' nostrils flared. "You have a nasty habit of esca-lating problems. You don't bring a nuke to a gunfight."

"Escalating? Nope. I end the shit I need to end, and I do it quickly, so assholes don't go on being assholes." James shrugged and looked at Nadina. "I'm not here to bust his balls. If he doesn't want my help, I'm fine with that."

Nadina rubbed the bridge of her nose. "Cyrus, I don't want James' help because I'm concerned about your performance. Let me make it very clear that I respect you and your team. I'm viewing him more as an unexpected resource. One who happens to be the strongest proponent of barbeque on the planet, and…" She sighed. "I apologize, James, since this is going to sound totally self-serving, but if something does happen and this becomes any sort of media incident, your involvement has good symbolic and PR value. If people hear that James Brownstone helped me, it might deter a future incident."

Cyrus' expression softened. "Using his reputation could work to our advantage. I see what you're saying."

James frowned. He didn't want to get in the middle of an internal work struggle, but walking away because the other guy was being pissy didn't suit him either. "All those people I saw outside aren't your normal team, are they? I've never seen Nadina travel with an entourage that big." He nodded at Cyrus. "I didn't even see you earlier. You were in the back?"

"I was coordinating things from the security office, yes," Cyrus replied. "There are cameras everywhere in this place. Several of our drones, too." A lopsided smile appeared, a hint of pride overcoming the suspicion in his eyes. "It's not like we need that level of hardware all the time, but we wanted to be ready for the big event. And you're right about the guards; we've got a lot of temporary contractors right now. The core team is a lot smaller, with me and a small group of rotating bodyguards working as Nadina's personal protection. We have security at individual restaurants as needed, but it's usually just a couple of guys at most. Everyone ultimately reports to me, but it's not like I need to tell guys at individual restaurants to wipe their butts, and most of the threats are targeted directly at Nadina."

"You have dedicated security for barbeque restaurants?" James furrowed his brow. He was having trouble processing the idea, but Nadina using her magic to boot out an unruly customer might not play as well reputationally as James growling at a guy and ordering him out.

"You've been to several of her places." Cyrus gestured with both hands. "All big places, and all popular, but because of *who* she is. She gets the whackos, whether they love her or hate her. They also don't always realize where she might be. You have to understand that she doesn't like to make too much trouble for the local police."

Nadina shrugged. "It's the price of fame. I've found that if I shoulder it more directly, it improves my relationship with the authorities, and I can better call on them when I actually need to rather than wasting their time with every man who wants to offer me flowers."

"When you actually need them?" James asked. "You mean, like now?"

"I will admit I'm slightly surprised the local police aren't being a little more aggressive in their response. It's kind of a loop. I didn't explain it in detail earlier, but the locals don't want to get too involved unless the FBI does, and the FBI, based on what they told Cyrus, feel that if the local police aren't worried too much, there's no reason to get more involved." Nadina stared into the distance. "Maybe it's all an overreaction. If the authorities aren't more worried, it might be silly that I am."

Cyrus shook his head. "Complacency is what gets people hurt."

James looked at Cyrus. "The FBI gave the locals all the information they need?"

Cyrus nodded. "Yes, but if the cops had the resources to handle all crimes, they wouldn't need people like bounty hunters, now would they?" His voice dripped barely concealed contempt.

*I know this guy thinks I'm making him look like a pussy in front of Nadina, but he should get the fuck over it.*

"Your guys," James began. "What's their training?"

"All well-trained. All ex-military or ex-police. I'm ex-AET myself."

*Is that why he doesn't like me? He thinks I'm some leftover threat who should have ended up in an ultramax years ago?*

James nodded, deciding to let it go. Maria had hated his ass when they'd first met, but had ended up working for him for years. The AET experience meant Cyrus had dealt with some of the same kinds of threats James had, and the bounty hunter could respect that. It meant Cyrus wouldn't panic in a firefight.

"You ever deal with LA AET?" James asked.

Cyrus shook his head. "I spent most of my career in DC."

"Okay. Forget about that. Was just wondering if you knew some of the people there." James' gaze lingered on a subtle line in Cyrus' jacket marking a concealed holster. "What kind of gear do your guys have?"

"We've got stun rods, stun rifles, conventional rifles, and sidearms." Cyrus' voice became easier. "We've also got access to sonic grenades when we need them, and anti-magic bullets and deflectors if we have specific magical threats. Every man who works for me has unarmed combat training, too. These aren't Rent-A-Cops, Mr. Brownstone. These are highly trained personal-protection specialists. This is why no one dangerous has ever gotten close to Nadina."

James glanced between Nadina and Cyrus. "Any magicals on the team other than your boss?"

Cyrus shook his head. "No. That's not really a concern."

James frowned. "How do you figure?"

Cyrus rolled his eyes. "You're thinking like a bounty hunter, Mr. Brownstone."

"Cyrus, please," Nadina begged. "He's only trying to help."

Cyrus sighed. "What I'm getting at is that Nadina's not being hunted by crazed magical criminals. Oricerans don't care that she's into barbeque. All the hatred comes from the human side, and even then, most of our threats are just overzealous fans, or the occasional stalker convinced Nadina should be his wife. That kind of thing." He sucked in a breath. "The HDL and other groups like that might make noise, but other than their stupid little speeches, we've never had anyone from those kinds of organizations come after her directly to hurt her." He smiled at Nadina. "And it's not like she's defenseless. She *is* a Light Elf."

Nadina smiled back.

"One anti-magic bullet from a rifle could kill her," James rumbled. "Knowing magic and having experience in life-or-death battles aren't the same thing. I'm sure you took down a few magicals during your time in AET because they didn't realize that."

Nadina grimaced.

"True enough." Cyrus looked at her and James. "And this latest thing? It's a little more trouble than normal. We're usually the ones going to law enforcement, not the other way around, but they also admitted it could all be talk."

James grunted. "So, who's doing all the talking?"

"An HDL splinter faction who call themselves the Defenders of Hope. They've not assassinated anyone, but they have bombed Oriceran-owned buildings in different parts of the country, Canada, and Mexico. People have been hurt, but not killed, and the Defenders haven't made it sound like they were sorry about it. They claim they'll never kill a human being, even a 'species traitor.'" He shrugged. "But it's hard to know with terrorists. The HDL is supposed to be non-violent too, but they keep breeding groups like the Defenders."

James pulled out his phone and brought up his bounty-hunting app. "And those assholes who were here the other day didn't say they were with them?"

Cyrus shook his head. "No. At least online, they have disavowed any violence and any connection to the militant HDL factions."

James perused the information on his phone with a few swipes. The most important piece was highlighted in a bounty summary field.

**Organizational [LIVE] Bounty: Defenders of Hope [US STATE DEPARTMENT-DESIGNATED DOMESTIC TERRORIST ORGANIZATION] Level 3.**

James snorted. A level-three bounty was barely worth Trey's time, let alone his, but at least it gave him an excuse to get involved. He wouldn't just be some do-gooder trying to solve an acquaintance's problem. This would be an official job.

"What is it?" Cyrus asked.

"They've got a bounty, but it's not as high as I would have expected." James slipped his phone back into his pocket. "So if they're involved, it'll be pretty easy to clean up."

*I think I'll wait to tell Shay about this. Not sure if she'll be pissed that I've been doing so much bounty work on my road trip.*

Nadina pursed her lips. "The question remains whether I should cancel tomorrow."

"What's going on tomorrow?" James asked.

"I've got a charity event at a local youth center, barbeque for the kids. I've thought about pulling out, but they're depending on me, and this is supposed to help with donations. I'm donating too, but I don't want them to lose out." Nadina shook her head. "The Defenders wouldn't attack anywhere children might be, would they?"

"You should go," Cyrus insisted. "We have it under control."

James cleared his throat. "I'm not an expert on this kind of thing, but spooking you might be their whole plan."

Cyrus nodded. "He's right. If the FBI and police don't think it's a big threat, it might just be that the HDL is talking trash to get you frightened."

Nadina sighed. "That makes sense." Her phone rang, and she pulled it out of her pocket. "I need to take this." She nodded at the door.

Cyrus opened the door and stepped out. James stood and followed. The security chief closed the door behind him once he was out.

"I'm not going to pretend I'm all that happy about you being around, Mr. Brownstone," Cyrus explained. "But if your presence can help keep Nadina safe, I won't bitch too much."

James grunted and shrugged.

"Nadina's going to leave town in a few days for a quick trip to Europe. This will all probably turn out to be nothing." Cyrus managed a smile, but its vulpine quality set James on edge. "And you can go back to LA."

"Don't worry. If these HDL fucks get anywhere near Nadina, I'll make them understand why nobody fucks with a pitmaster."

Cyrus laughed. "You're a strange man, James Brownstone."

James shrugged. "I've been called a lot worse."

## CHAPTER SIXTEEN

"You're shitting me," Shay exclaimed over the phone, then snickered. "Sometimes I think there's a god of mischief hiding behind you who likes to mess with you."

James had returned to his hotel room and decided to call his wife, despite his earlier thought to keep his plans to himself. Upon reflection, he returned to one of the main lessons he had learned in his years of marriage: lying by omission never worked out in the long run, regardless of the reason.

"Happy wife, happy life" might be a cliché and easy to ignore, but most men's wives weren't retired ex-killers or tomb raiders with short tempers and access to deadly magical artifacts.

James now sat on the edge of his bed, his phone in hand, finishing his explanation.

"Nope." James grunted. "Those HDL fucks I saw protesting the other day might be annoying, but if they had the balls to do something to the building, they already would have. The Defenders do have an organizational bounty, so I might as well put in some local effort. The cops seem reluctant, for whatever reason."

Shay chuckled. "So let me get this straight: you're staying in Denver not to enjoy barbeque, but to hunt down a terrorist group for a bounty? I know you helped Trey because he asked, but this isn't exactly what I had in mind when I said you should take a road trip."

"That about sums it up. You're saying you're pissed?"

"Not at all. You don't sound stressed, and that's my only real concern. It's hard to tell with you and ass-kicking. Sometimes it relaxes you, and sometimes it just pisses you off more." Shay sighed. "I'm hoping this doesn't mean you'll need another road trip after this one to think about the baby again, though. That was supposed to be the point, rather than you defending the honor of barbeque from all who would besmirch it." She offered the last few words in an atrocious English accent.

James smiled. "No, the road trip helped with the baby."

"It did?" Shay sounded cautious yet hopeful.

"Yeah. I'm not saying I'm never gonna wonder about anything going forward, but all this barbeque stuff made me realize I have something great I can share with the kid. Alison was too old to be raised as a true barbeque lover."

Shay laughed. "So I tell you that I'm having our child, and you're all concerned about whether you can handle it, but now you're excited because you'll have a barbeque buddy?"

"Yeah. Basically."

"Sometimes I wonder if Whispy engineered that barbeque obsession into you for some strange reason only he understands," Shay replied, a hint of disbelief in her voice. "You've been changed so many ways, but the core of the man always remains."

James furrowed his brow at the thought. He had rarely communicated with his symbiont about anything food-related. Whispy only cared about power, and that meant he only cared about magic items or the increasingly few times that James became furious while bonded.

*Nah. Not everything is a Vax-symbiont conspiracy.*

"Fine," Shay muttered. "Just so we're on the same page. How long do you think you'll be staying in Denver? It's not like I need you right away, but you know how sad Thomas gets when you're gone. It's like he thinks I'm sending you off to fight demons every time you're gone for more than a day."

"I figure it'll only be a few more days. You know how these kinds of assholes operate. They want media attention, and if they wait too long, they might lose the chance to be the big story since there's always some asshole blowing something up somewhere. I'll poke around, but I don't even think it'll be that hard, and that's if someone's actually trying something, and they aren't all talk."

"And if they *are* trying something?" Shay inquired.

"Then I kick them through a few walls," James rumbled. "Those guys are a bunch of pussies who like to hide. Once I find them, I can end them."

"Uh-huh." Shay sighed. "I don't care that you're doing this since I want you to have a good time, whatever that means, but I do think I have to point something out. I don't want you pissed off later."

"What?" James frowned.

Shay took a deep breath. "If you blow up Nadina's

restaurant, you'll be doing the terrorists' work for them. I know you'd pay to fix it, but her business will lose momentum, and people might stop going out of fear. You've dealt with terrorists before, but usually, you've gone after them on their turf or somewhere that didn't matter much if it got damaged."

James scoffed. "I'm not blowing up her restaurant, and I'm not letting anyone else blow it up either. If there's a fight, it'll be somewhere else. I'm gonna make sure of that." He nodded firmly to himself. It wasn't like he *always* destroyed a building.

*We didn't total the golf course. I mean, there was what? A couple of major craters? They can fill that shit in easily.*

Years ago, the Council had attacked James at a restaurant, and although the owner had benefited from the publicity in the long range, James suspected Shay was right. Any action against Nadina's place didn't have to do major damage, it just had to plant the seed of fear. The HDL, ironically, was only constrained by their concern about collateral damage.

*Fuck it. I'll just have to find them first.*

James let out a low growl. "I'll remember everything you said, but it's late, and you should get some rest."

"The baby isn't going to pop out early because I'm up a little late, but I am tired," Shay replied. "Okay, I'll talk to you later. I love you, and do try to keep the collateral damage to a minimum. You're supposed to be retired, remember?"

"I remember, and I love you too. And I always... Uh, okay, sure. I'll try." James grunted.

Shay ended the call, and James set his phone on the nightstand.

A small smile broke out.

*Maybe I needed an ass-kicking road trip as much as a barbeque road trip—just a little exercise where the stakes aren't so high, unlike what happened with Alison, or even Trey. This isn't about stopping a dangerous drug from flooding a city. It's just about finding a bunch of assholes who have it coming and showing them who they should really be scared of.*

---

A half-hour later, James flipped through the channels on the hotel tv. He had intended to go to sleep, but fatigue eluded him despite the long day. After a few channel changes, he stopped when he spotted the word "local barbeque restauranteur" in a news chyron. James turned the volume up and read the full text.

**Local pitmaster takes issue with Nadina.**

James narrowed his eyes.

A white-haired man was showing a reporter around a grill in the back of his restaurant as a voice-over played. His wrinkles deepened as he smiled.

"Many people know Atticus Taylor as 'the Pork Wizard,'" the reporter explained in a voiceover. "He has been part of the Denver barbeque scene for over twenty years. He opened his first restaurant after leaving behind a long career as a financial manager. Dissatisfied with his career and financially secure, he decided to step away from his old job and pursue a lifelong passion: barbeque."

The image changed to a direct shot of Atticus sitting in

a chair, competition trophies arrayed on a table behind him, chatting with a relaxed and easy smile.

James had heard the guy's name at competitions, but he wasn't one of the top pitmasters in the scene. That didn't necessarily mean anything. Some people only liked to cook and didn't like competitions, but the trophy table seemed to imply otherwise. The shot wasn't long enough for James to identify any of the trophies.

*Might just be a news story, but it kind of pisses me off.*

"Could you give us your thoughts about the recent protest in front of the Spice and Spell?" the reporter asked with a serious expression on his face. "None other than pitmaster and former bounty hunter James Brownstone has made some very strong public statements about it."

James grunted. He was surprised no reporters had tracked him to his hotel.

Atticus let out a long, weary sigh. "This is America, the land of opportunity, and to have these men come here and protest her because of her species just isn't right." He clucked his tongue. "They should be ashamed of themselves. That goes against everything I believe in as a man and a pitmaster."

James nodded. *Damn right.*

Atticus frowned. "But that doesn't mean there are no issues to be considered with the opening of this restaurant. And I want to be clear: I've been talking about this ever since I first heard she was going to open a place here. I've got statements online from six months ago."

The camera shifted to a shot of the reporter nodding.

Atticus raised a finger. "Local businesses mean stronger investment in the local economy. I'm from Denver, and I have an investment in this city. Not just as a place of business, but as a place I call home. I never had any children, so my barbeque career is kind of like my child."

The reporter nodded. "I don't understand. Are you saying Nadina shouldn't be able to open a restaurant here or that she should?"

"It's not that she shouldn't. I'm saying she's a celebrity. She's been on several shows, and not just *Barbeque Wars* years ago." Atticus shook his head. "While I'm sure her barbeque tastes fine, she's leeching customers from other local barbeque places, and I'm not convinced the quality of her food is higher than some of the other local places she's going to harm. It's unfair competition."

"You're saying you feel her place is going to hurt Denver barbeque restaurants?"

Atticus considered his words for a few seconds before responding. "I'm saying there's a good chance of that, yes. I'm not saying this because she's an elf. Regardless of her species, if she had been born and raised in Denver or I thought she was going to relocate to Denver, I wouldn't mind because I would know that her intention was to build up this city. But she lives in New York." He made a face. "New York," he intoned again as if the mere invocation of the city's name was all the proof he needed of Nadina's unsuitability as a Denver barbeque restauranteur. "This latest restaurant is just part of an empire for her. How is she going to help Denver?"

"Her business will be paying taxes," the reporter suggested. "And some of her staff are locals."

"True, but how much money will she donate to local schools? How much attention will she pay to local politics?

167

We need to build up local businesses and community, not let *outsiders* come in and disrupt us." Atticus sighed melodramatically, as if he couldn't believe anyone didn't see the obvious.

The reporter gave the other man an incredulous look. "Aren't you worried about accusations of hypocrisy?"

Atticus frowned. "What do you mean? I don't think it's hypocritical to raise questions about Nadina's restaurant, and I still feel the HDL protest was inappropriate."

"What I'm talking about is the fact that you yourself run a chain and have financial interests in restaurants outside Denver, including several others in Colorado, along with places in Utah and Kansas. In addition, your company recently opened a restaurant in California."

Atticus took a deep breath. "That's a fair response, but it's not the same thing. The situations are different."

James grunted. *How the fuck isn't it the same thing?*

"Oh?" the reporter asked. "Could you clarify that for us?"

"Of course." Atticus licked his lips. His mouth twitched, and a hint of anger appeared in his eyes. "My first couple of places were opened here in Denver, and I push local Denver eateries all the time. I've located my new places in areas that aren't being served by existing barbeque places. I would never *knowingly* harm another barbeque place."

The reporter nodded slowly. "The owner of Flaming Volcano Barbeque in Provo might disagree. You opened a place within a half mile of his restaurant, and he's had to file for bankruptcy."

Atticus waved a hand, clear irritation on his face. "The owner there has made several false statements about my business practices. I should note I might be filing a lawsuit against him soon. Predatory pricing? Illegal restraint of trade? I can't believe he actually accused me of messing with his suppliers. What nonsense! You shouldn't be spreading his lies."

The reporter raised an eyebrow. "I didn't mention any of those charges."

Atticus stood. "This interview is over."

James turned off the tv. The whole thing was irritating to him. He laid his head on the pillow as he considered the Pig and Cow.

Atticus claimed he tried to avoid other barbeque territories, but James had actually done that. The closest other pure barbeque place to his had gone out of business a few years after he opened the Pig and Cow, but as far as he knew, that had far more to do with the original owner dying and poor business practices by his son, including spending a lot of his revenue on dust and other drugs.

James couldn't be sure. He did get a lot of business from tourists and people way outside the neighborhood. One man came up from San Diego every couple of weeks. James might not be a celebrity chef, but he was still a semi-retired world-famous bounty hunter, and there was no doubt that he had a few advantages most people didn't when starting a restaurant. It helped that he had managed to stumble into one major incident a year that garnered him some media attention, and that was setting aside everything Alison did to keep the Brownstone name in the news.

*Not every restaurant can survive, and sometimes good food isn't enough. Is that fair? No, but life isn't always fair, and if someone has good skills, they can always go work for someone else's restaurant.*

*But at least a place deserves a chance to fail, not to have terrorist assholes threaten them and get them to close.*

James reached over to turn off the light next to the bed. The best food should rise to the top, and he wasn't going to let terrorists prevent that.

# CHAPTER SEVENTEEN

The next day, James leaned against the wall in a cavernous gym connected to the youth center, his arms folded over his chest. Peals of children's laughter made him grunt. He might now be looking forward to his own child, but it didn't mean he was all that comfortable around other children.

*Maybe that shit will come with time, but I doubt it. It's not like Shay and I are gonna be hanging with the PTA discussing the best way to do fundraisers for the school trip and shit.*

The more James thought about it, the more he had to face the fact that his experiences with Alison hadn't prepared him for a new child. Besides her age, she'd spent most of her last few teenage years in a boarding school. James felt he had done a good job, but he'd spent a large amount of time training her to be a bounty hunter. Her sense of family loyalty was already firmly established before they had even met.

James shook his head. None of that had to be a bad thing.

*So God gave me an easy kid the first time. That should mean I'm ready for the greater challenge on round number two.*

A young boy broke away from a group playing tag nearby and scampered over to James, his eyes filled with the hope and innocence only young children could manage. He smiled brightly, revealing several missing front teeth before fishing a crumpled piece of paper and a pen out of his pocket. "Can I have your autograph, Mr. Ghost? Nadina already gave me hers. It's so fancy."

James glanced down at the boy. Apparently, his feeble attempt at a disguise—sunglasses and a Colorado Rockies cap—didn't help. He had been trying to stay away from the kids, worried that he might scare them.

The boy held up the paper. Nadina's elegant signature scrolled across the crumpled paper.

*At least I know this kid isn't gonna sell this shit online.*

"My name isn't Ghost," James rumbled. "It's Brownstone."

The boy's only smiled wider. "Can I have your autograph, Mr. Brownstone?"

With a grunt, James took the paper and signed it before handing it back to the kid. The child promptly scurried back across the gym, which was filled with tables and chairs.

At the front, piles of ribs, brisket, and grilled chicken sat on trays. Nadina appeared from a kitchen in the back, a smile on her face, flanked by two assistants holding more trays. Adults and children sat scattered around the tables, chatting happily and gobbling barbeque.

Nadina took a moment to chat with a few of the kids who were picking up food before returning to the kitchen. Her assistants remained behind to continue serving.

*It's a youth center for kids to hang out, not an orphanage, but it reminds me a lot of where I grew up.*

Other tables stood in front of a temporary stage. They held piles of baskets filled with donations for an auction later. Security was scattered around the exterior, most looking bored. Nadina had asked the organizers of the events if they wanted to cancel, but after some reassurances from the local police that there was no specific threat, they had decided to go forward with it, citing James' presence as a deterrent.

*Maybe there really isn't a problem. The cops and the FBI aren't dumbasses. This might be nothing but HDL blowing hot air in the end. If one of their groups attacked a building full of kids, they would never be able to hold one of their little protests again.*

A few children ran by. While Nadina was just helping out a youth center for at-risk kids, not an orphanage or a group home, it was hard not to see himself in the young children running back and forth. The priests at the orphanage had helped ensure he grew into a good man, or if not a good man, at least not a total piece of garbage. Considering his true potential, they might have very well saved the world.

*If they hadn't helped me give a shit, would Whispy have taken over the first time I went into advanced mode? I lost my shit. I was hacking away at those fuckers long after they were dead.*

James frowned as he remembered all the times he had let rage overtake him while bonded. Whispy fed on it and helped him maintain it, creating a feedback loop. That made sense, given that it was being used as a power source.

*Was I risking everything all those times before I convinced Whispy to change his primary directive?*

If Whispy had taken control, James would have summoned the Vanguard, and Earth would have been helpless. Even the best-case scenario involved the Alliance showing up and solving the problem by bombarding major cities and killing millions if not tens of million, and that was unlikely. And if not the Alliance, then the government, who would deploy nuclear weapons or strategic-level magic.

Everything James understood about the Alliance's fleet presence during the Battle of LA suggested they had brought the ships because of him, and they'd only had time to do that because the Shepherd had been aware of him. He didn't know anything about how quickly the Alliance could send their ships across the galaxy, but he doubted they could snap their fingers and get a bunch of ships there in hours. That was one of the reasons they feared both the Vax and magical portals.

*Someday in the future, Earth will be on even footing with the Alliance, but if I'm still around, they'll never trust this planet. They should spend more time looking for the Vax homeworld than freaking out about me.*

James grunted, wondering if the Vax were hiding from everyone now. It wasn't like the Alliance was dropping by his restaurant to have a little brisket and discuss galactic warfare.

Three new kids ran James' way with pens and paper. A smattering of adults who had finished their food now wandered around the gym, moving chairs into position in front of the stage. The actual event for donors and the community didn't start for another hour, and a few of the higher-level media representatives wouldn't be coming for thirty minutes.

James walked across the gym, smiling at the children. He accepted that he had held onto the wrong mindset the entire time. When Shay had told him about being pregnant, he'd focused on how complicated it would be to raise a kid rather than accepting that he already knew what it took to raise a good kid from a young age. He had the perfect model in the priests who had raised him.

It wasn't as if James believed everything would proceed without stress or failure. There would be bullshit, yelling, and mistakes, but there was nothing to fear.

*I can do this. Shit, Shay and I can do this. It's just another change in our life, and one for the better.*

A shrill fire alarm cut through the air.

"What the hell?" James muttered.

Several of the children shouted in surprise and looked around, fear suffusing their faces. Some of the adults stood, brows furrowed in confusion. Nadina's assistants grabbed the hands of some nearby children and ran for the exits.

The rest of the adults hopped to their feet and began pointing to the emergency exits. The children rushed that way, many screaming.

James frowned and looked around as people fled the gym.

*Is this an actual fire, or just some kid thinking he's being funny?*

The lights cut out, leaving the gym lit dimly by stray

light streaming through the high windows. The alarm died, but the staff continued evacuating the kids.

*False alarm, or is the fire in the electrical system?*

James sniffed at the air and looked at the kitchen. There was no sign of smoke, and no one was coming out of the kitchen. A few of the security guards rushed that way. One pointed to his ear as he murmured something to another, but they were too far away for James to make anything out.

Cyrus rushed into the gym past a stream of fleeing children. He grimaced, looked around for a few seconds, and sprinted toward the kitchen.

*What is going on?*

James searched the main gym one last time to ensure there were no children left behind. The staff had corralled the few kids who hadn't run for the exits. They had the evacuation well in hand, but one thing still bothered him and pricked at the back of his mind, refusing to let it settle, and not just Cyrus sprinted toward the kitchen.

*I don't smell or see any smoke.*

Cyrus threw open the door to the kitchen and hurried inside, anger on his face.

James jogged toward the kitchen. He patted his amulet but decided against bonding.

Someone shouted from inside the kitchen. James kicked open the door and prepared to charge, raising his hand and ready to reach inside his shirt to pull off the spacer separating his amulet from his chest.

Cyrus stood near a counter, his teeth gritted. He stood in front of several security guards. He glared at James before turning back toward the men. "Go to the perimeter and physically check with everyone. Make sure. Don't assume."

James let the door close behind him and looked around the kitchen. The tempting smell of grilled meat saturated the air, and multiple open grills stood near the back of the narrow space. Several kitchen tools were scattered on the ground next to a tray and ribs littered the ground as if someone had tossed them there. A scorch mark marred the back of the tray. Nadina's cracked phone lay on the ground near the tray.

His gaze drifted to the back door. There was half a large bloody handprint near the handle.

"I don't need any help, Brownstone," Cyrus muttered through gritted teeth. "This situation is well in hand. Get out of here."

"The situation is well in hand?" James looked around. "Where's Nadina?"

"The situation is well in hand," Cyrus repeated.

James squared his shoulders and glowered at the other man. "I didn't fucking ask that. I asked where Nadina is, asshole."

Cyrus swallowed and averted his eyes. "We're checking on that."

James snorted. "'Checking on that?' She was just here." He pointed to a back door. "Did you check out there?"

"I'm not an idiot, Brownstone." Cyrus stared at James as if deciding whether to continue. "We have reason to believe Nadina is no longer on-site." His shoulders slumped.

"What?" James narrowed his eyes. "What the fuck does that even mean?" He pointed to the downed meat, the tray, and then the door. "I might not be some fancy-ass body-guard or detective, but it fucking looks like to me there was a fight in here."

"We do believe there was a struggle." Cyrus licked his lips. "There's a possibility that Nadina's been kidnapped." He pointed to the door. "One of my men is unconscious on the other side, but not dead. They must have surprised him so they could come in through the back."

James stared at Cyrus for several seconds. "You're fucking terrible at your job."

Cyrus frowned. "We don't have time to sit around pointing fingers. I've got my people checking everywhere. If the kidnappers are on foot, they'll spot them. I will recover her and them."

James shook his head, wondering if he should punch the man for his incompetence. "Check the cameras. This place has to have cameras. We need to figure this shit out."

Cyrus rolled his eyes before reaching into his pocket and pulling out his cell phone. He tossed it on the counter next to him. "Whatever you think of me, I'm not blind enough to ignore the obvious."

James glanced at the device. "What? You already have the camera feed set up on it?"

"No. Didn't you notice? The lights and alarm died at the same time." Cyrus tapped a receiver in his ear. "Our comms died, too. We think someone EMPed the building."

James pulled out his own phone. It remained active, but it'd been hardened against normal EMP attacks, something Shay had insisted on after an incident in Bahrain a few years back when she thought he was dead because he hadn't been able to call her for a day afterward.

Cyrus gestured toward the door leading to the gym. "I'm having some of my people go to the men on the perimeter to call the cops. This is a security situation, Brownstone, not a bounty-hunting situation. Maybe if your daughter was here, she might be able to help, but I'm going to be honest: we don't need a thug pitmaster's help, and you'll only get in my way."

James snorted. "If she got nabbed by the Defenders, she doesn't have a lot of time. The only thing holding those fucks back is concern about killing humans. They aren't going to have a problem killing a Light Elf. We might not have a lot of time."

Cyrus flung a hand in the air. "You think I don't fucking know that, Brownstone? Why don't you get the hell out of here and let me do my job?"

James shook his head and turned around. He didn't have time to waste in a dick-measuring contest with Cyrus. The conversation was pointless. He pushed out of the kitchen. The cops had obviously underestimated the HDL, but so had the security chief.

*Fuck. I underestimated them too. I thought if they did anything, they'd come in here trying to make a big show, not sneak in the back. Subtle assholes are the worst assholes.*

*Fine. I'll let the cops and Cyrus do their thing, and I'll do mine.*

# CHAPTER EIGHTEEN

James stepped outside and marched away from the gym. He glanced at the lines of children arranged far from the building, some looking terrified, others excited. Adults were counting the children, and the few parents there were pulling their own children into embraces.

There was still no smoke or fire.

*It was all just a fucking misdirect. Great. Just fucking great.*

Sirens sounded in the distance, along with the flashing lights of incoming fire trucks. Drones from both the fire and police departments hovered overhead, circling the area.

*If the HDL had the resources to EMP the damned building, they aren't going to stick around. Cyrus was too damned slow.*

James turned toward his truck, which was in the parking lot. If the HDL had fried the truck, he might have to reconsider the live part of the bounty as well as figure out some other way to get around town. He suspected

Nadina didn't have more than a couple of hours left at most.

A quick jog brought him to his vehicle. James slipped inside, and the engine started with its normal roar. The console display came to life. He grunted in relief.

James set his phone to speaker and dialed a number he hadn't used in a while. He took a deep breath and slowly let it out as the phone rang.

*I don't have to like someone for them to be good at their job.*

"Woah," answered a man's voice. "I always get nervous when the dude himself calls me. It makes me think something's about to blow up, brah. Good timing. I just finished eating my tofu wrap. You really should try this stuff. You'll live way longer than if you keep eating all that grilled meat."

Davion sounded like a surfer, but as far as James knew, the man hated the water.

"I don't have time to talk about that shit." James grunted. He missed Heather every time he had to deal with Davion, but he was happy she had left the agency to start her own cybersecurity products company. Maria and Trey both swore up and down that Davion's skills justified his eccentricities, particularly since he was an infomancer and could bring magic to hacking, which put him above both Peyton and Heather.

"Okay, okay, chill. I was just offering a suggestion."

James had agreed to hire Maria and Trey when he'd retired, so he wasn't about to undermine them by saying they should fire the man for being annoying and anti-barbeque, no matter how badly it offended him.

"It's work time, not food time," James rumbled. "And I

need your help. Nothing's gonna blow up. Some assholes might die, but first I need to find those assholes. Hard to punch someone when they aren't anywhere near me."

"You ever try yoga, brah?" Davion replied. "I mean, I get that you're James Brownstone, but maybe you just—"

"Like, I don't have time for this shit," James growled. "And it's important, so fucking pay attention."

"Damn. Touchy. It's okay. I'm not busy. I was running down some background checks for Maria, but it's nothing that can't wait. Anything for the man whose name is on the building—not that I'm ever in that building." Davion chuckled. "What did you need? Did some dumbass threaten you or something?"

A firetruck turned a corner and rolled to a stop in front of the building. Several firefighters stepped off and walked toward a gesticulating staff member. Two of the firefighters moved toward the hose, uncertainty on their faces. Several more red and white drones lifted off from the back of the truck, small silver tanks of fire retardant underneath.

"I'm in Denver," James explained, watching the firefighters with a frown. "For the opening of Nadina's new restaurant, but I'm at this charity thing. Whatever, that shit's not important. The important part is, Nadina probably just got kidnapped by an HDL terrorist group called the Defenders of Hope."

Davion gasped. "Woah, brah. Where did she get kidnapped from?"

"From the building I'm parked right outside of. You can trace my phone. Her phone is still here." James gritted his teeth. "I need leads ASAP. If we wait for her security and the cops, she might end up with her throat slit. Her security chief allowed too many holes in her security. The HDL bastards EMPed the area, so I'm doubting the cops are gonna be able to get anything off local cameras, but the cops also don't have you."

"Damn. That's some intense shit." Keys clacked in the background. "Rescuing a hot kidnapped celebrity? Does Shay know?"

"Just fucking do it," James growled. "This is important. She's a friend, and this is about barbeque."

---

Davion tormented James with his offkey humming for the next few minutes as he continued his efforts without any complaint. The same laidback nature that rubbed James the wrong way also made the man always happy to do his job, even in stressful situations.

*I know he can find her. I just need to be ready.*

James had pulled out of the parking lot and was on his way back to his hotel. The cops might have had questions for him, but their procedures would slow things down, and the local police didn't have access to resources like a highly skilled infomancer. This wasn't an investigation; this was a race.

"Huh. That's kind of weird," Davion reported. "Kind of annoying, too."

James stopped at a red light and looked around the area as if he would get lucky and see a bright yellow van with HDL KIDNAPPERS written on the side zooming past instead of just some asshole in a Lexus and a scared-looking teenage girl in a car with a STUDENT DRIVER sign.

"What's annoying?" James asked, drumming his fingers on the wheel as he waited for the light to turn.

"Well, she's famous, right, brah? Nadina. And I'm thinking these HDL dickwads aren't friends with a lot of high-powered magicals, so I figured I'd just make this shit easy and track directly with a little of the old magic." Davion sighed. "But no dice. Damn. I can't home in on Nadina with a straightforward tracking spell. If I got my hands on something personal and important to her, I might be able to rig a short-range directional tracking spell, but, uh, you're, like, there, and I'm, like, 'Yeah, that's not going to work.'"

James accelerated as the light turned green, his jaw tight. "There's personal shit I can get from her, but you're right. We don't have time to mess around. If they're blocking your tracking spells, that means they do have a wizard."

"Maybe. A few of the militant HDL cells have got a few wizards to help them, but that shit's rare."

"It's not a big deal. I can take down wizards easily enough." James hoped it was a wizard. Straightforward enemies provided straightforward targets.

Davion sighed. "I'm betting it's not that. Sorry, brah, but I'm guessing they're using an artifact to block things. There's no way for me to tell from here, but that's what my gut says."

"Damn. I was worried about that."

"Why is an artifact worse?" Davion asked. "It can't set up counterspells—not that I couldn't handle them."

James took a hard turn, his tires squealing. "Because it's probably easier to keep it near her without needing a guard near her, which gives them flexibility. She's not just some pitmaster, she's a Light Elf. There's a risk of her waking up and doing magic, like undoing the blocking spell."

"Totally. I can see it. Not to be, like, a total downer, brah, but why do you think they've just knocked her out instead of, like, totally killing her ass? Not saying I'd be happy. That'd be a big waste, but these are anti-Oriceran terrorists, and they don't agree."

James grunted, his hands tightening on the wheel. "I thought about that at first, but it doesn't make sense. I don't think she's safe, but we have at least a small window to save her."

"I know normal HDL might not be about killing people, but these militant splinter groups like the Defenders can get nasty. Did these guys say anything that makes you think they are going to try to ransom her or something?"

"I wish." James grunted. "No, nothing like that. I think they plan to kill her, just not right away." He frowned. "These guys had the resources and plans to distract everyone. This wasn't a bunch of dumbasses just charging in and dropping bombs. They didn't even kill the security guard, even though they surprised them. They set off that alarm, but they then EMPed everything, which means they had reason to believe they could set the alarm off without being seen."

Davion chuckled. "That's easy. That just means they need a computer dude who's not a total dumbass. You don't need magic to hack most systems, and that's going to be true for a long time."

"Yeah, I know. I'm just saying they were careful about all this shit. More careful than I would have expected. It's not like I expected them to bomb a youth center, but gunning down a security guard and then gunning down Nadina in her kitchen and filming it would have accomplished their goals."

Davion sucked in a breath. "Dark, brah. This is why I like it when the agency goes after normal criminals. Greedy, uptight guys are easier to relate to than those crazy terrorist nutters."

"All of what I said keeps forcing me back to the same idea."

"The same idea? Shower me with wisdom, brah."

James changed lanes, his brow furrowed in thought. "All that shit means the Defenders have a lot of resources, and if this were just about killing Nadina right away, why not just kill her in the gym and leave her body for us to find? They might be terrorists, but they're obviously not dumbasses. They have to know that taking her means her security, the cops, and I are gonna come after them hard, and right away."

"True enough," Davion replied. "You sure they didn't kill her and are just going to dump the body somewhere?"

"When you've killed as many people as I have, you learn a thing or two about bloodstains."

Davion snickered. "James Brownstone, Forensics Master."

"Yeah." James grunted. "There was a little blood in the building, but not enough to make me think anyone's dead. They must have some other plan. I'm thinking they've got her, and they're taking her somewhere else. They *are* terrorist fucks, so they probably want to make a propaganda video or some shit *before* they kill her, and that's the window we have to exploit. It'll take them time to drive to wherever their hideout is and film things. I might be wrong, and they might decide to hold her for a day and wait for things to calm down, but I'm not willing to bet Nadina's life on it."

"That shit's still pretty bad, brah. I mean, it's cool that she's probably still alive, but this doesn't sound like it's going to end all happy-like."

"Yeah, it won't...for the Defenders," James growled. "It also means we have time, just not a lot. Do your job, and I'll do mine. If I come after them and they haven't already killed her, they'll probably keep her alive."

"How do you figure?" Davion asked.

"They know they can't win against me," James explained. "So a hostage is the next best thing."

"Not like you can knock down a building if she's in it," Davion observed.

"I'm not knocking down any buildings this time. I'm just gonna kill all the assholes inside them." James' nostrils flared. "Do what you can. You know how to do your job better than me. I'm gonna hang up, but call me once you have something I can use. I don't give a shit *how* you get the information. Just get it quickly."

"Will do, brah."

---

James frowned at a passing police car. The cops hadn't bothered to call him, but Cyrus had probably gone out of his way to discourage them. Maybe the police had found some subtle clue that had eluded him and were on their way to rescue Nadina. He didn't care as long as it ended with captured or dead terrorists and a freed pitmaster.

His phone rang with a call from Davion and James narrowed his eyes. It had been twenty minutes since he'd delivered his orders. Instead of returning to the hotel, James decided to circle the youth center with an increasing radius in the feeble hope that he might run across anything suspicious.

*Time to prove the power of tofu, Davion.*

"What do you have for me?" James answered gruffly.

"I've got a location," Davion responded, pride filling his voice.

"Shit." James almost slammed his brakes in surprise. "Really? I thought you couldn't track her."

"Damn. That hurts, brah. Have some faith. I'm not just about the magic. Shit. I'm mostly not about the magic, and I'm not saying I can track her. I'm saying I used my sweet skills to figure out a location for a suspicious van that sped away from the back of the youth center. They loaded her into the van from what I can tell, but they were carrying her." Davion chuckled. "Okay, so that's kind of tracking her, but not the way you meant."

"Suspicious van?" James echoed. His early hope had been closer to reality than he anticipated. "And you know where the van is now?"

"Yes. I know exactly where it is." Davion took a deep breath. "Yeah. You see, I went and did a filter algo on a bunch of satellite images for the area. It's not enough to get close images, but I could clearly make out them carrying and loading someone into the van, and I assumed it was her. So I started cross-referencing the times and then taking that data—"

"I don't care about any of the technobabble shit," James snapped. "Just tell me where the van is."

Davion rattled off an address. "It's a house. I hacked a nice drone, so I can tell you there are thermal traces of people inside, but the building doesn't have any active internal cameras to hack, and they're keeping the blinds closed, so long-range cameras aren't helping. Straight-up, though, brah, there's something weird about the house. My magic keeps getting blocked. So if they do have an artifact, it's a little stronger than I thought, and it might be general anti-magic. Even if Nadina's conscious, she might not be able to do much."

James snorted. "Not a problem. Anti-magic artifacts might contain an elf, but they're not gonna do shit against me."

# CHAPTER NINETEEN

U*nlikely the enemy will present a significant threat or opportunity for adaptation,* Whispy complained as James turned off the main road into a subdivision. *Select stronger enemies for maximum adaptation. Inefficient use of resources can result in the development of poor tactical habits.*

James had pulled off the road a few minutes prior to bond the symbiont before continuing toward the address Davion had given him. He'd stayed with basic bonding. His armor wasn't necessary yet.

*That sounds a lot like you saying, "Practice like you play, but only against quality opponents,"* James sent. *Don't worry. Sometimes it's fun to go through fuckers and not have to worry if I'm gonna blow up half the city. All these people keep giving me shit about blowing up buildings.*

*Collateral structure damage is irrelevant,* Whispy insisted. *And sometimes necessary for destruction of enemies. Destruction of enemies is of paramount importance.*

James snickered.

*Yeah, I don't think people will buy it if I tell them it's not important if I blow up buildings as long as I win. Don't worry. I'll make this shit quick. I'll take those bastards out, grab Nadina, and head to the cops so they can protect her rather than that dipshit Cyrus. That guy couldn't protect a baby cow from a bored vegetarian.*

GRANT ACRES WELCOMES YOU declared a large sign near a bubbling fountain. Thick algae choked the fountain. James hoped they weren't paying high HOA fees.

He didn't spot any other cars in the subdivision, or anyone doing yard work. The fewer people around, the more he could cut loose if necessary. Taking down the kidnappers quickly would not only satisfy Whispy, but it would also reduce the danger to Nadina.

*Shit. This is why bounty hunting is less obnoxious than security work. I don't know how Alison puts up with having to protect and find people all the time. I would lose my damned mind if I had to do this kind of thing much.*

James had considered calling the police, but he preferred to be able to handle the terrorists in whatever manner he saw fit. Depending on what they'd done, the situation could easily shift. Nadina might not be a close friend, but she *was* a friend, and that meant an attack on her was an attack on him.

It would be easy for James to send a message to people that they shouldn't screw with anyone even tangentially associated with him. Considering how many people still screwed with Alison, though, the lesson hadn't reached all corners of both worlds.

*The fuckers should have watched the news. Everybody in Denver knows I ran off those other HDL fuckers. Doing this while I'm still in town is like them asking me to show up and beat their asses. The only thing further they could have done was sent a handwritten invitation.*

The F-350 coasted to a stop across from the target house, an unassuming blue ranch fronted by a verdant lawn. Dark curtains concealed the inside. A long driveway flanked the lawn. Apparently, the Defenders liked their basic subdivision living style.

Something about the house annoyed James. It wasn't like he had been expecting a textbook evil hideout, but the presence of the otherwise normal house served as a reminder of the kind of dangerous scum who could be lurking around innocent people.

*Always wolves hiding in the woods, huh? They should have stayed hidden.*

James pulled his .45 and took a few extra mags from a concealed compartment under the glove box. Even if the terrorists had some sort of anti-tracking artifact, he doubted they had anything that could hurt him.

They wouldn't have been sneaking around otherwise. The basic reality was that if someone was capable of taking down James, they were capable of taking down the local AET and other bounty hunters without too much trouble.

James grunted. This would be quick if the terrorists didn't immediately surrender. He wasn't all that concerned about a payout. He almost felt sorry for the bastards. Almost.

The door flew open, and several scowling men poured out with large rifles.

*Okay, not going to waste time with bullshit games where you pretend you're just a normal house. I can work with that.*

James chuckled. The terrorists' eagerness assured

him that he didn't have to waste any time verifying if this was the right place. Kicking down some poor bastard's door who was just minding his business might have led to a police misunderstanding. James was always aware that not all departments trusted him as much as the cops in LA and Vegas, but he didn't have time to forge personal relationships with the police department of every major city in the United States.

"Fine. They want to play, then let's do this shit." James threw open the door and jumped out of the vehicle, running several yards to put distance between the truck and him. If the Defenders opened fire, he didn't want his truck to take any hits. Every time he needed it fixed, there was more risk they wouldn't be able to, and he wasn't convinced Oriceran mumbo-jumbo repair spells or potions would be able to repair his truck.

Men continued coming out of the house.

"This doesn't have to end with you all dead," James shouted. "But it fucking will if you don't surrender right now. You assholes know who I am, and you know what I'm capable of, so give it up and give me Nadina."

A total of eight men emerged from the house, all pointing their guns at James. He slowly walked a few more yards away from the truck until he stood in the middle of the street. A glance over his shoulder revealed a FOR SALE in front of the house behind him. The blinds were open, and there was no furniture inside.

The empty house, combined with the lack of other vehicles or signs of habitation, suggested that as long as he kept himself between the two houses, it lowered the chance of a stray bullet hitting anyone. Sometimes a man just got lucky.

James snickered at the realization that the empty house was going to get shot up. Maybe he wasn't so lucky.

Everyone was right. He couldn't handle the situation without some building getting damaged, even if he wasn't the one who would be damaging it.

*I'll cut whoever owns it a check when this is all over, but it's not like I can invite the terrorists to an empty field.*

The men exchanged looks, some uneasy, some angry.

One of the men took a step forward, his weapon pointed straight at James. "Turn around, Brownstone, and go. This has nothing to do with you, and we have no beef with you." His voice wavered at the end.

*Yeah, this isn't about saving me. It's about saving you. You're right to be afraid, asshole. It just might save your life.*

James shook his head. "It's definitely my fucking business. Nadina's a friend of mine, and shit, I might do this kind of thing even if it involved some prick like that Atticus Taylor. You don't fuck with barbeque. I don't care about your reasons or your philosophy or whatever. All I know is that you fuckers have Nadina and I want her back. Everything else is just irrelevant bullshit."

The gunmen exchanged confused glances. James didn't care if they understood his reasoning as long as they accepted that *he* believed it. The risk to Nadina increased with every bullet fired.

"You're seriously not going to back off?" the man who had spoken earlier inquired. "This isn't a bounty situation."

"Sure, it is. Level three on the Defenders of Hope."

The man's face twitched. There was uncertainty in his

eyes. James wasn't quite sure about the thought process, but anything that might get him to surrender was fine.

James shrugged. "I'll make this shit easy for you. I don't even need you to surrender. You can all leave. I just want Nadina."

"Take him down!" screamed the man.

*Fucking moron. I tried to give you an out, but you still had to be a dumbass.*

The men all pulled their triggers, and the loud crack of burst-fired rifle rounds disrupted the peaceful quiet of the suburban neighborhood.

Birds shot from trees on several nearby lots. Some of the windows in the house behind him were shattered by bullets that missed James. If there was anyone actually at home in the neighborhood, they would soon be calling the police.

*Don't have a lot of time,* James thought as the first few bullets struck his chest and arms. *I don't want to have to spend time convincing the police I should be involved.*

*Then maximize killing efficiency,* Whispy suggested.

*It's a live bounty. I should at least try to not kill them, right?*

*Incorrect. Primary mission is female recovery. Eliminate the enemy with maximum efficiency.*

Having Whispy was like having Jiminy Cricket on his shoulder, if Jiminy Cricket were a homicidal sociopath who saw everyone else in the world as nothing more than a tool for making James stronger. But in this case, the symbiont was correct.

*Good point,* James responded. *Fuck it. I was thinking that earlier anyway.* He grunted as a bullet bounced off his head.

Without his armor layer, the shots hit him directly, but

they accomplished little other than a sting and leaving a few scratches or the occasional mild laceration. The shallow wounds began healing immediately, small silver-green tendrils extending to knit the skin closed, leaving only a few bloodstains here and there. The sad reality for his enemies was that having eight men firing assault rifles at him was simply an inconvenience.

*Fuckers are gonna have to do a lot better than bullets if they want to have a chance against me.*

*Maximum adaptation to attack type already achieved,* Whispy reported. *Kill useless enemies with maximum efficiency or end battle through other efficient method. Remember primary mission of recovering female.*

*Hey, not every battle can be special,* James sent. *Sometimes we just kick the ass that's in front of us. When you reach the championship, there are just gonna be fewer teams who can keep up with you.*

*Teams are irrelevant. Please note, use of symbiont is unnecessary for low-level foes.* Petulance flavored the thought.

James snickered. Whispy was right, even if he obviously just wanted to finish a fight that wouldn't end with additional adaptation material for him. Sitting there getting blasted by terrorist losers was pointless. It was time to grab Nadina.

With a grunt, James whipped up his pistol and squeezed off three quick shots. Two men's heads exploded and a third fell to the ground, his hand over his chest as blood blossomed from the new hole.

*You assholes should have at least worn bulletproof vests. Offense with no defense gets you dead damned quick.*

The surviving men ceased fire, indecision on their

faces. The earlier speaker glared at James, his eyes burning with hatred.

James sighed. "About now, you've got to be thinking, 'Hey, we just put a hundred bullets into this fucker, and he's still standing and doesn't look messed up except for his clothes.' If you're *not* thinking that, you should be, because I'm sure a few of you are also using anti-magic bullets and are really surprised that they aren't doing shit against me."

Two of the surviving men glanced down at their rifles, their mouths tight.

"If those were your big plan, you've failed." James shrugged. "If it's not clear, I'm James Brownstone, and I've taken down a lot tougher fuckers than you, but you're in luck. If anything, it's your luckiest fucking day ever."

"Luck?" one of the men called back, incredulity flavoring his voice.

"Yeah, because I don't really give a shit about you or your stupid terrorist bullshit," James rumbled. He nodded toward the house. "I know you brought Nadina here, so drop your weapons and hand her over. That's the only way you walk out of this breathing. Your bounties aren't even that high, and you're terrorist dipshits, so I don't care whether you survive. Choice is on you, but I want it very, very clear that if this ends with you all dead, I'm not gonna lose any sleep, and I doubt anyone in Denver will either. They're just gonna go on the news and say, 'James Brownstone kills terrorists.'"

The men exchanged looks. One of them swapped in a new magazine, his eyes narrowed.

*Kill the enemy,* Whispy insisted. *Kill the enemy!*

*I can't kill them all. I might need them for a code or some shit like that. They might have weird restraints on Nadina.*

*Kill the enemy. Symbiont disruption of restraints possible.*

James' eyebrows lifted. Whispy had a good point, but he couldn't be sure. They might have placed a bomb on Nadina, and disarming bombs by the typical Brownstone method would probably involve a large explosion.

*Damn it. Why can't shit be simple? Nothing sadder than a stubborn idiot about to die.*

James patted his bullet-riddled shirt. The few minor scratches and abrasions on his body had already healed. "Here's the thing," he shouted. "I don't give a shit about your grand mission or rants or whatever. You get that, right? I'm not going around the country kicking HDL ass. I'm supposed to be retired, and I'm supposed to be having a relaxing road trip focused on barbeque, not people kidnapping pitmasters. Do you have any idea how many pieces of shit there are in LA?"

The men blinked. One man shrugged. Another man offered a guess of two hundred.

"There are a lot, that's my fucking point. Plenty there with bounties are getting taken down, but plenty who are just garbage don't have bounties or my attention." James grunted. "Because they mind their fucking business, so they don't end up dead." He waved his gun. "These days I only come after people as personal favors, in defense of friends and family or in defense of barbeque. It just so happens in this case, we've got all three going on." He took a menacing step forward. "Now, I'm done talking. Hand over Nadina or get ready to go to Hell."

"Full auto!" screamed of one of the men. "Waste his ass! We just have to whittle down whatever shield he's using."

*You poor, stupid bastards.*

The garage door groaned and began to rise.

*More reinforcements? Or are they trying to run? Shit, they might be running with Nadina.*

The men flipped their fire selectors and pulled their triggers. Bullets swarmed James like he had kicked over a large wasp's nest. More glass shattered behind him, and wood cracked. The projectiles ripping through the house showered wood fragments all over the front.

The sheer volume of shots forced James back, leaving scratches and abrasions all over his unarmored body and further shredding his shirt. It was little more a few thin scraps now, and his embedded amulet was visible.

The garage door continued opening to reveal a dark van with tinted windows. The cloud of bullets shots made it difficult to pick out targets. Difficult, but not impossible.

*I need to end this shit. They're just trying to stall.*

James growled and put two rounds into each man. The last two survivors backed away, uncertainty on their faces as they swapped in new magazines and continued firing, only to die a few seconds later when he shot them in the head.

He'd given them chances only because he was worried about Nadina. They had chosen to die.

After tossing his gun to the ground, James yanked a small magical coin out of his pocket, another Shay treat, and slapped it against the amulet. The tendrils shot from Whispy to cover his body and combined to form his armor. He'd briefly considered using it before, but losing a shirt wasn't as wasteful as using a magical artifact to fuel a transformation.

It had been a long time since he'd been able to summon the rage necessary to transform without a Shay treat, but it'd been a long time since someone had done something as spectacularly idiotic as threaten Alison or Shay to his face. Even when he'd gone after the dark wizards, he had felt more irritation than anger.

The van shot forward and zoomed down the driveway, bouncing after going through a small dip separating the driveway from the street.

Extended advanced was overkill for a bunch of fools with probably nothing better than anti-magic bullets, but he needed to take out the van before they escaped with his friend. Firing his .45 at random might end with Nadina getting hit, and he doubted her kidnappers had put a shield around her. They hadn't intended to use her as a hostage or human shield, but that didn't make her any less of one.

James' transformation was complete about the same time the van hit the street. He didn't bother with a helmet since he couldn't spare the few seconds it took his eyes to interface with the expanded vision system of the armor.

The van rumbled as the driver made a hard turn. His effort left a streak of rubber when he floored it, and the vehicle shot forward.

*No, you don't, asshole. You're not getting away.*

James leapt, his enhanced legs propelling him high into the air and right toward the fleeing van. He retracted his arm blade as he closed on the back of it. Stabbing where he couldn't see was too risky. He had no idea if Nadina was lying down or sitting up, or where she might be in the van. Time for other options.

With a roar, James landed and raked the top of the van, his claws sparking as they sank into the now-dented roof. The vehicle accelerated, but no fireballs or gunfire blasted through the roof. No strange swords or spears, either.

*This shit won't end like that thing in Barcelona. Do they not know I'm up here? The roof is dented. They have to be able to see that, or maybe Nadina's tied up in the back by herself.*

James bounced as the vehicle turned, but his claws anchored him it. With a growl, he tore into the roof and yanked it open. He dropped into the back of the van, expecting an imprisoned Oriceran pitmaster and maybe a few terrorists or a bomb.

There was nothing in the back but some road flares and a few stray shell casings.

*What the hell? Those idiots have the hostage up front?*

Kneeling, James frowned. He climbed back onto the roof and flipped himself onto the front of the van, his claws gripping the side and top of the front window. He was now close enough to see inside despite the tinting.

A scowling man sat at the wheel. He gritted his teeth, raised a pistol, and began firing. Cracks spiderwebbed from the impact holes, and the bullets bounced off James' armor. There was no one in the passenger seat or the back seat, which raised an obvious question.

*Where the fuck is Nadina?*

James lunged and smashed his clawed, armored hand through the windshield to rip out the throat of the terrorist. The man slumped forward on the wheel.

The van jerked, turning so hard that it flipped on its

side, sparking and crunching as it scraped the road. Glass fragments from the side mirrors littered the asphalt, sparkling in the sunlight.

James let go of the now-defunct vehicle and hit the street, the collision barely registering through his armor. He rolled several times before hopping to his feet with a growl, trying to figure out what the hell had gone wrong. Had the van been a distraction? Was Nadina still in the house?

He jerked his head around, but he didn't see any other vehicles other than a newly arrived police drone flashing red and blue circling high overhead.

Another mighty jump sent James back toward the house. Sirens sounded in the distance, but he didn't care. The local police weren't going to mind that much that he'd finished off a few terrorists.

*Surprised they didn't rant about their big manifesto like that idiot at the protest.*

With a loud thud, James landed in front of the porch. He kicked in the door, expecting more enemies, but there was nothing inside except leather furniture and a few empty bookshelves.

*They've got to have her stashed somewhere, and I'm not waiting for the cops.*

"Nadina?" James bellowed. "It's James. Are you here?"

The only response was the quiet hum of the air conditioner.

James charged around the house, throwing or kicking open each door, whether room or closet. Two large metal crates filled with rifle magazines occupied the master bedroom, but otherwise the house looked like any other reasonably furnished suburban home, and it conspicuously lacked his missing Light Elf pitmaster.

James growled. "What the fuck is going on?"

Lights flashed from the outside as multiple police cars pulled up. James grunted and ignored them before popping open the entrance to the attic and poking his head inside. The insulation looked like it needed some work, but Nadina wasn't there either. There was no basement in the house.

*Well, shit. Now I wish I hadn't killed everyone. I've got no fucking leads.*

*No additional adaptation gained during encounter,* Whispy reported. *All damage regenerated. Combat efficiency remains maximal. Efficiency improvements recommended for future encounters of similar nature.*

James grunted. "This kind of thing is why I retired." He stomped toward the front porch. Multiple police officers had out their weapons and were crouched behind their vehicles, anxious expressions on their faces. Considering the bodies littering the front lawn, that wasn't unreasonable.

Their eyes widened as the armored bounty hunter emerged.

"Put down…" a cop began, then blinked. "Wait. You're James Brownstone."

"Yeah, I'm James Brownstone." He nodded toward the house. "Don't worry. There's nothing left to do because there's no one left alive. I was looking for Nadina."

The cop nodded. "And?"

"And nothing," James growled. "She's still missing."

# CHAPTER TWENTY

James stared up at the ceiling fan in his hotel room, his head resting in his hands. Nadina was still gone, and he had no idea where to even begin looking. Every minute that ticked by meant more danger.

Davion was running his algorithms and filter spells on camera and drone recordings, but he'd already confirmed no other vehicles had left the house or the neighborhood during the fight. The van couldn't have been a distraction if they weren't covering for anyone.

*I fucking missed something. Maybe those guys never thought they could beat me. They stalled me. Did they portal her out of there?*

James frowned. If the kidnappers had that kind of magic, they wouldn't have had to rely on some of the tricks they did, and he doubted they would have tried to stop him with a few rifles. Alison could probably give him a decent fight if she went full-out, and even she couldn't open portals on command.

No. There was something else.

The whole thing was like a sauce recipe missing a key spice. Something was missing, something that would make everything come together and point to the location of the missing elf, but he couldn't distinguish the flavors well enough to figure out the missing ingredient.

The police were equally clueless. They had taken a brief statement from James before letting him go. They still needed to verify that the dead men belonged to the Defenders of Hope, but they had already explained that James' violation of the live capture requirement meant he would likely get only a small fraction of the money, if any. They weren't planning to arrest him since it was clearly self-defense, but they didn't like the fact that he had killed everyone.

James didn't care about the money. The bounty had been an excuse to justify getting involved originally, but now that the terrorists had made their move against his friend, the pocket change wasn't important. His only regret was that he had no one left to interrogate.

*I assumed she would be there. Why wouldn't she be there? It's not like they left her at the youth center. The cops are still all over that place.*

"Fuck." James sat up and curled his hands into fists. What had he missed? The kidnappers had grabbed Nadina at the youth center. The security teams had been patrolling the building and outside. Maybe the kidnappers had hidden in a car in the parking lot and waited for their opportunity, but that meant there was a good chance of a cop or security seeing them. That sort of plan seemed too risky.

*Maybe I should start carrying a spare receiver. If I had been in touch with Davion, he might have been able to help me.*

James sighed and shook his head. Most of the incidents he had stumbled into since retirement were more straight-forward than finding a Light Elf pitmaster who had been kidnapped by terrorists. The more extra equipment he carried around, the more he risked slipping back into being a bounty hunter and not a pitmaster.

*I left the agency and the job behind. That part of my life is supposed to be done, and now I've got a new kid coming. That's even more reason to not get drawn back into worrying about shitbags by default, but none of that helps me find Nadina right now. Fuck.*

*I went straight to that damned house. It still hasn't been that long since I killed the Defenders. If they don't have her on a plane and they didn't use a portal, she still might not be that far away. I just have to find out where.*

The thoughts lingered in his head for a few minutes before James' phone came to life with a call from Davion. He picked it up and brought it to his ear. "You calling because you got something? I'm not in the mood for bullshit."

"Yeah, brah. I got something you'll like."

"And what's that?"

Davion took a deep breath. "There was a second vehi-cle. A car."

"So the van was a distraction, but I thought you said... who cares." James stood and frowned. "Okay, a car left from the house. Can you follow through cameras or satel-lites or some shit? I just need to know where they are."

"No, no. You don't get it. I was right before. No one left the house or the neighborhood during your fight. The second car left the youth center after the van. I just tagged the van first, so I concentrated on it, and I didn't even think about another car leaving." Davion groaned. "Shit. I wonder if they planned that on purpose. They might have worried that security would catch on, so they offered the van as bait."

"So it *was* a distraction, just not the kind I thought?" James frowned. "Do you know where the car is now? These people are trying to be too cute, and that means they're leaving themselves room to make a lot of bad mistakes."

Davion sighed. "Yeah, I know where the car is, but there are a few weird things about all this. Things that make me kind of worry, you know?"

"Like what? I'm not worried about the Defenders. Their best efforts accomplished exactly jack and shit against me. Just point me at them."

Davion clucked his tongue. "Okay, so, the van was like what you'd expect. It was stolen. They changed the plates, but the cops ran the VIN and figured it out. The car was different, though. The car was one registered to Nadina's company, not stolen or anything. It was a vehicle the security team had used for a while."

"So what? Where is it now?"

"The problem is the car drove downtown and stopped in a covered alley and never came out. I sent a hacked drone over there to check, and the car's still there. Only residual thermals, by the way, brah." Davion blew out a breath. "Not to be a freak, but even if she was dead in the trunk, it hasn't been long enough. I'd still be able to pick up her heat. Trust me, I've been in that kind of situation before. I guarantee she's not in that car. If she was? I don't know, but she's not there now."

James grunted. "We can't be sure she was ever in that car, and she wasn't in the van, so we basically don't know any more than we did before. That's useless."

"Sure, but she's got to be somewhere, right?" Davion chuckled. "And stealing one of her company's cars has got to mean something."

"Yeah, the fuckers kidnapped her and stole one of her cars too, which means they were taking on more risk." James shook his head. "That takes balls, but maybe they figured it'd look better for some stupid-ass propaganda video. They must have taken her from the car and transferred her to another vehicle, or they've got her stashed in a building near where they ditched the car. Was there a door near the car?"

"Yeah. The alley's next to a big office building. There are thirty different companies in there, and it's ten stories. That's a lot of real estate to cover. If I start trying to hack everything, it might cause a lot of trouble, and it'll take a while. I'll do it if you want, but I'm not sure that is the best way to handle this."

James considered driving over to the building and just marching into the lobby, but he doubted Nadina's kidnappers controlled the entire building, or any of it. If he spun up thirty companies, the cops and the FBI wouldn't help, and James didn't even know if she was there.

*At least I have a lead now, but I need to narrow this shit down. There's got to be something else he can tell me.*

James frowned. "You're right. They might have just transferred her to a different vehicle. Wasting all our time without being sure isn't the best play. You got anything else for me? I'd tell you to dig more, but we don't have enough time to fuck around."

"Oh, maybe it's not the best time to tell you, but they've already got an ID on one of the guys you took down, and it's kind of weird. Maybe that's useful somehow." Davion chuckled. "I decided to take a little stroll through the Denver PD system just in case, by the way. I kept totally under the radar, but just be aware that's how I got the info. Anyway, the guy they IDed isn't known to be associated with the Defenders or HDL. From what I can tell from a quick check, he's a freelance dirtbag from Chicago who does kidnappings, hits, that sort of thing. He did a few years in prison, but he's been out for a while. Why would the HDL hire someone to help them? Did they need more muscle? I can kind of see it, but these ideological terrorist groups don't tend to do that kind of thing. A lot of criminals hate terrorists."

"Maybe they didn't hire him. People get radicalized in prison all the time." James frowned. "He might be new to the HDL, and he's just not been in long enough for the local cops or FBI to have gathered info that he was a recruit."

"Yeah, yeah. Probably. Maybe? It's not like regular criminals never become terrorists, but like I said, he's been out for a few years, and it's not like I did a deep dive. But just checking on what the police records say, this guy has never been associated with the HDL. And that's not the only weird thing. There are just too many dangling strings with this, brah."

"Then what else do you have?" James asked. "Anything that can lead me to Nadina is helpful."

Davion sighed. "I don't know. Maybe it's nothing, but I think one of the reasons the cops didn't seem as interested in Nadina is they were getting a bunch of tips in the last week from an informant claiming the HDL wasn't planning on messing with Nadina, and that it was just a diversion so they can totally screw up some big Oriceran sister-city dinner the mayor has coming up."

"Huh?" James grunted. "Who's the informant?"

"Don't know. The cops don't know, and it seems like they weren't that convinced of anything until the HDL filed for the protest permit. The informant told them about it before they showed up. I poked a little, and I'm kind of freaked out. Maybe not freaked out, but I'm like, 'Woah. That's freaky.'" Davion chuckled. "Same thing, huh? I'm reminded of this one time in San Diego—"

James growled. "Get to the fucking point, Davion."

"The point is, I was able to geolocate the source of one of the messages from the informant."

"And?"

"Whoever their informant was, they made at least one call from inside Nadina's place before it opened," Davion explained. "That means some HDL asshole might have been distracting the police while they were placing a bomb in her restaurant. It's all, you know, 'Look at this hand' as a distraction while they're grabbing the knife with the other. I could be wrong, but it fits the evidence."

"You're right about it being weird, but a bomb doesn't sound right." James walked over to the window and pulled back the curtain to reveal an unimpressive view of a parking lot and a few nearby local restaurants. "If they had a bomb, why didn't they already set it off? They could have done it at night when no one was inside if they were worried about killing humans. It doesn't make sense. The longer they wait, the greater the chance of someone finding it."

"I don't know. I don't belong to an HDL terrorist splinter group. You've dealt with a lot of terrorists. They're not always like, you know, reasonable. I mean, they're terrorists. They need to chill, but they just like blowing shit up."

"Being reasonable isn't the same thing as being logical," James replied. "If they were total dipshits, they would all get caught by the government right away. No, if they planted a bomb and haven't set it off yet, there would have to be a strong reason. And I'm assuming Nadina's people were sweeping for explosives, especially since bombs are the Defenders' weapon of choice." He grunted. "But if it was a magical bomb, they might not know what to look for. That still doesn't answer the question of why the Defenders haven't set it off yet. No, there's something else here you haven't found."

"Sure, brah, but what?" Davion sounded more curious than offended.

*Unless...*

James narrowed his eyes and pulled the curtains closed. "I need you to check something for me, Davion. I hope I'm wrong, but if I'm right, it'd explain a lot of the strange shit about this situation and give us a chance to track down Nadina."

"Okay," Davion replied. "What do you hope you're wrong about, and what do you need me to do?"

"About how complicated this shit may be, and here's what I need you to do…"

---

An hour later, there was a loud knock on the hotel room door. James marched over to the door and opened it. Cyrus stood on the other side with an annoyed look on his face.

James walked back into the center of the room and stood near the bed. "Thanks for coming on such short notice." He folded his arms over his chest and tried not to look pissed. It was harder than he had thought it would be.

Cyrus entered and closed the door. He looked around for a few seconds before declaring, "Sometimes I wondered if your reputation was bullshit, but apparently, it's not. Who knew?"

"My reputation? How does looking around my hotel room tell you anything about my bounty-hunting reputation?" James frowned as he tried to connect the two in his mind, but he failed. "I mostly hit bounties in greater LA. I wasn't a big hotel guy back then."

"I'm not talking about your bounty hunting." Cyrus gestured around the room. "You have your one little restaurant, but you have been taking down level four and five bounties for years. That's a lot of money. You could have retired to a tropical island well before you stepped back from bounty hunting." He shrugged. "And you still live in a small two-story house. You do have that ridiculous truck, but the point is, you're in a midrange hotel here, not a luxury place, despite attending the opening of a celebrity restaurant. Humble living for a rich man."

"Humility is relative, considering some of the stuff I use and have." James shrugged. "But why would I need a luxury hotel? I just need somewhere to sleep. My wife's not even with me."

Cyrus stared at James, his gaze appraising. "Whatever. I was trying to be nice, but I'm not here to discuss you, Brownstone. You dragged me over here and claimed you had vital information about Nadina that you couldn't share over the phone." He shrugged. "I'm here. Tell me. You of all people should understand that time is running out. We're just fortunate they didn't assassinate her at the event. We might get lucky and they intend to ransom her, but we can't depend on that. You know how terrorists are."

"Yeah, I do, and that's the thing."

"What do you mean?"

"It was an inside job," James explained. "I don't think the HDL had anything to do with Nadina's kidnapping. Any of them—Defenders, normal HDL. I think those fuckers just showed up for their protest, and it has been used to help distract from the real kidnappers." He held up a hand. "You know, like a magic trick. Keep your eye on the ball and all that shit."

Cyrus scoffed. "Wait, so you're saying she kidnapped herself?"

"No. That would be stupid. I'm saying someone from your team did. Maybe multiple people." James narrowed his eyes. "Or maybe one person."

*Eliminate enemy,* Whispy recommended. James had bonded the symbiont a few minutes before and told him to be quiet, which in practical terms translated only to fewer kill requests.

Cyrus shook his head. "Bullshit. I personally vet everyone on my team, and I've used the subcontractors before. They're professionals. There's no way it was my people. I take full responsibility for what happened, but that doesn't mean it was an inside job. I don't have time for this, Brownstone. It won't help me or the police find Nadina."

"Yeah. I figured you would say something like that, which is why I had someone check into you for something very specific." James' nostrils flared, and he resisted the urge to punch the man across the room.

"Check into me?" Cyrus' face twitched. "What the fuck is that supposed to mean?"

James squared his shoulders. "Exactly what it sounds like. I had someone check into your accounts and see if you got any recent payments. It took a little digging, but my guy found it, or at least can link you to a crypto wallet that received a shitload of TrollCoin a week ago. I don't understand all the technobabble, but he says you have other accounts linked to that. He hasn't traced it all back yet because he didn't have a lot of time, so I don't know who paid you, but it was a decent amount. Not enough to retire to a tropical island, but enough to compensate you for the fact that your boss isn't supposed to come back. You can go take a vacation for a few months until the news dies down, then get a new job."

Cyrus scoffed. "This is complete bullshit. Have you lost your fucking mind, Brownstone? Nadina's out there, and terrorists have her. She might already be dead, and you're running around playing at being a detective. You're a pitmaster and a bounty hunter, Brownstone. Stay in your fucking lane and stop being an idiot."

"I don't have to be a detective to smell shit that stinks or spot someone acting suspicious." James shook his head. "That's what's been bothering me about this situation from the beginning. Nadina's not an idiot, and she's a pretty good judge of character. I couldn't understand why her security chief would let her get captured so easily, which means normally you must do a good job, but the money explains why you suddenly stopped."

Cyrus gritted his teeth. "You were there too! They just surprised us. Shit happens, even when you're prepared."

"Yeah, shit happens, and yeah, I was there," James growled. "But I was backing off because you were being a little bitch about it, and you were right. I'm not a security contractor like my daughter. I don't guard people most of the time, but a lot of the shit you did still didn't make sense to me, like the single guard at the back. It was like you were asking for someone to screw with her. If you had changed a few things about the security, they couldn't have gotten to Nadina and run off with her."

Cyrus snorted. "This is insane. Batshit-crazy. I don't have time for this, Brownstone. I can't believe you're wasting my time with these bullshit conspiracy theories." He turned toward the door. "Stay out of this, Brownstone, or I'll go to the cops and have them arrest you for harassment. I'll admit I got a little desperate and thought you might actually be able to help, so you can add that to my list of mistakes, but I'm not stopping until I rescue Nadina."

James chuckled and offered Cyrus a tight smile. "You

seriously think I'm letting you walk out of here?" He shook his head. "I don't know what the fucking plan is, but you're gonna take me to Nadina. Or you can say no, and I'll break every bone in your body until you tell me where she is."

Cyrus glared at James. "You think you're so fucking smart, don't you, Brownstone? You're not smart. You're rough, and that's why I have an advantage over you."

James grinned. "I'm smart enough to have seen through you, asshole."

Cyrus pulled out a gun. "I stuck an anti-magic magazine in this thing before I drove here, asshole. I told you to stay out of this. Fuck you." He fired.

# CHAPTER TWENTY-ONE

Cyrus pulled the trigger three times, his face a mask of crazed glee. The bullets ripped through James' shirt and bounced off, barely stinging.

*Maximum adaptation already achieved. Unlikely the enemy will present a significant threat or opportunity for adaptation,* Whispy noted. *Disable, extract intelligence through whatever means necessary, and kill.*

*Nah. We stick to the plan.*

Cyrus blinked and glanced down at his gun, then back up at the smirking James.

"You know what the sad part is?" James rumbled. "I thought you might show up with a grenade or some shit." He slapped his chest hard, the shirt outlining the amulet for a moment. "So I put this on. I thought a little bit about playing dead, but it's just not in me, so too fucking bad, Cyrus."

Cyrus hissed and fired again. "Die, Brownstone. Die!"

James grimaced as a bullet bounced off his head. Despite another light sting, there wasn't any blood.

"I don't understand," Cyrus muttered. "These are hollow-point anti-magic bullets. Even if they weren't as effective as normal, they should be at least tearing you up a little."

"I'm sure they're fine. Too bad you spent so much money for nothing." James shrugged. "The problem is, everyone always assumes magic has something to do with my shit. There are other possibilities besides magic."

"What the hell are you talking about?" Cyrus' eyes widened, and his breath caught. He stood there frozen for a few seconds before turning and fleeing down the hallway.

*Pursue enemy!* Whispy demanded.

James pulled his phone out of his pocket. It was already connected to Davion.

"Cyrus is moving," James explained. "Make sure you keep on him in case he switches vehicles." He jogged out of the room. "I want to give him a little head start so he'll run where we need. He's in too far to just drop out now."

---

James pulled his truck into the parking lot of an abandoned warehouse on the edge of town. Despite his speeding, no cop had pulled him over. He wasn't sure whether that was luck or people not wanting to mess with James Brownstone. He would take it, either way.

*Shit's working out the way I want it to for once. I just hope it ends with Nadina being okay.*

Cyrus had pulled in through a loading bay door a few minutes prior, according to Davion. The dilapidated warehouse didn't look like a base of operations, with its broken windows, peeling paint, and graffiti.

That simplified things since it implied Cyrus and his buddies weren't involved with some local Mafia, which had deep ties and resources. There was still a chance they might be affiliated with the HDL in some way, but if that were the case, the man wouldn't have needed a bribe to betray this employer.

"I'm leaving my phone in the truck," James explained. He'd been in constant contact with Davion on speaker during the pursuit. "I'm going extended advanced. I don't have time to fuck around, and last time I tried to bring a phone with me and grew a little pouch, it got fried anyway."

"Understood," Davion replied. "And good luck, brah." He cleared his throat. "Cops are at the hotel now looking around. They'll probably figure it out sooner rather than later, but do you want me to call them?"

"No. I can't wait, and they will want to do this too slowly, or they might have a problem with me getting a little rough." James snorted. "Nope. I'm ending this shit, and I'll clear everything up with the cops later. I'll call you when it's done, but this ends now."

"Sure, sure. Kick a guy through a window for me." Davion laughed. "Damn, it's always fun working with you. I wish I had been at the agency before you retired."

James grunted. "Talk to you later." He ended the call and pulled out a Shay treat from his pocket, a small piece of turquoise etched with a single rune. It was a healing artifact under normal circumstances, but now it'd be nothing but fuel for Whispy.

Even if James managed to make money on the job, the reward wouldn't offset the value of the artifacts he'd drained to fuel his transformations. While he didn't regret that, it was a strong reminder of how expensive things could get when the heavy violence started.

*Cyrus should have given up on his plan the minute I got involved. He underestimated me, and now he's gonna pay for that, and for betraying Nadina.*

James took a moment to pull off his clothes. No reason to waste another outfit. The bullet-riddled shirt couldn't be saved without magic, but at least he could wear it while driving.

Not caring who might see him, the naked James stepped out of his truck with the sunken amulet in his chest and tendrils obvious. He slapped the turquoise to the amulet, hoping Cyrus and his friends were watching. Anticipation of death shredded morale, and everyone knew what James' armor represented.

*Let's go extended advanced,* James ordered. *Including helmet. We're gonna eliminate the enemy.*

*Yessss,* Whispy responded.

The Shay treat crumbled to dust, and a few seconds later, biometallic tendrils encased James' body forming an armored killing machine. A blade extended from his arm, and the darkness of the helmet surrounding his head was replaced a few seconds later by a wider field of vision.

James considered thermographic vision before deciding against it. If he made enough noise, the enemy would come to him, and that was assuming they weren't already watching him on a camera.

Hiding wouldn't save them. Attacking wouldn't, either.

They had sealed their fate when they'd fucked with his friend.

*Time to knock.*

*Kill the enemy efficiently,* Whispy commented. *Recover target.*

*That's the plan. I gave them all the chances they're gonna get. Now it's time for them to understand what it means to fuck with me.*

With a grunt, James leapt away from the truck and flew toward a rusty side door. He landed and grabbed the door with his now clawed and armored hand. His tug didn't open the locked door, so he backed up and slammed his foot into it, leaving a large dent and sending the door several yards into the interior hallway it had protected. The door landed on the dusty tile with a loud, echoing thud. If they didn't know he was there before, they knew now.

James cocked his head. There were shouts nearby from multiple men and he grinned, imagining them in a panic.

He jogged down the hallway toward the source of the noise. A few turns brought him onto the main warehouse floor.

Cyrus' car, along with a few other vehicles, was parked inside. A dozen men were present, most holding rifles, but several with grenade or rocket launchers. Most of the men wore gray fatigues. Cyrus had ditched his pistol for a grenade launcher.

*Who are these guys, mercenaries? So we've got Cyrus getting paid, and we've got mercenaries. Damn, someone spent a lot of money to go after Nadina.*

"That's a lot of gear to kidnap one Light Elf," James

rumbled. He gestured around. "We really gonna do this? I don't care, but you might like continuing to breathe."

Cyrus sneered. "You've fucking ruined everything, Brownstone. I'm going to have to leave the country after this." He gritted his teeth. "Why? Why? You never come to the fucking openings, and you chose *this* one to suddenly come to?" He groaned and scrubbed a hand over his face. "You damned bastard."

James shrugged. "I needed to take a barbeque road trip, and it ended up that Nadina's place was opening. So I'm gonna ask you again: where's Nadina?" He punctuated his sentence with a loud growl.

A few of the men exchanged nervous glances.

Cyrus licked his lips. "We can cut you in, Brownstone. This doesn't have to go down badly. Be reasonable."

James barked a laugh. "You said it yourself back at the hotel, dumbass. I've got plenty of money. I don't need yours."

"You look like a freak in that armor close up," Cyrus shouted. "I've seen it on the net, but you don't even have eyes on your helmet. But we've got a few tricks, Brownstone, and if you're not going to join the team, you're going to die. This won't be like the guys you killed at the house. We've got better weapons, and we weren't sure what kind of weird magic crap might happen, so we've got some interesting toys."

"This will go down exactly the same." James stepped forward. "Everyone's gonna die here today except you."

Cyrus snorted, something approaching hope in his eyes. "Oh? You want to work a deal with me?"

"No. I still have a few questions for you. But for

everyone else, it's time to die." James charged toward the flank of the enemy line.

Whispy's approval radiated into James' mind.

The loud, echoing sound of rifles spitting lead filled the room. The bullets bounced off James' armor without him even noticing. A rocket hissed away from one man's weapon and exploded against James, scorching the surface of his armor and knocking him to the side, but it only took him a few seconds to right himself. It wasn't deadly, just an inconvenience.

His enemies took the opportunity to back away. More rockets and grenades exploded around James, annoying him by blinding him with smoke and debris from the damaged warehouse floor rather than doing much against his armor. His thick biometallic coating reduced the deadly attacks to tickles, not even the stings from before.

*Maximum adaptation against all attack types*, Whispy reported. *No evidence of new adaptation potential. Increase efficiency of elimination.*

*Yeah, let's do that.*

James ignored the stream of bullets and jumped. He came down on top of a rifleman, the loud crunch of their collision weaving itself in with the cacophony of bullets. The man's scream died in his throat as James caved in his chest.

The nearby mercenaries backed away, including one man with a grenade launcher who had yet to fire.

James let out a low growl as another rocket exploded on him.

The grenadier raised his weapon. "Suck on this!"

Everyone else ceased firing as the man launched two grenades in rapid succession.

Both grenades slammed into James and splattered a viscous green liquid all over the front of his armor. He looked down, confused by what had happened. There was only a slight sizzle on his armor, but it ate away at the floor when it dripped.

*Oh, acid. That was their big plan? Pathetic.*

*Maximum adaptation already achieved*, Whispy reported. *Increased nullification and regeneration in progress.*

The sizzling stopped.

James shook his head and sprinted toward the acid grenadier. The mercenary's eyes widened, and he stumbled backward and raised his weapon.

James sliced his arm off. The man howled and fell to his knees, but his pain was short-lived since his opponent decapitated him a second later.

*Increase efficiency!* Whispy demanded.

The vengeful pitmaster didn't hesitate, bounding from man to man, stabbing, slicing, and ripping. Blood splattered the hard cement of the warehouse floor as each man died. Their few last attacks didn't even slow James.

Lip quivering, Cyrus dropped his weapon and ran for a hallway on the other side on the room. He reached into his pocket and muttered something under his breath.

*Keep running, asshole. It won't save you.*

James finished the last of the mercenaries with a final stab through a rifleman's heart. Cyrus turned a corner, his breathing ragged.

*Enemy boasts of attack potential have proven unfounded*, Whispy reported, irritation coming through the link.

*Seems that way. This shit is over. Cyrus just doesn't know it yet.*

James sprinted after the other man, the echo of his heavy footsteps bouncing around the cavernous room. He hit the hallway and turned the corner, half-expecting some weird demon or death wand, not an open door to a mostly empty storeroom with a few stray crates scattered about.

Nadina was tied to a chair at the back of the room, a gag in place. Her eyes widened as she spotted the armored James coming for her, and she struggled against her bonds.

James marched into the room. Four crystal-tip tripods surrounded Nadina. He was no expert, but he suspected they were anti-magic emitters similar to the ones Alison's enemies had tried to use on her.

*Anti-magic emitters? Bribes? Mercenaries? Someone had put a lot of money into this shit. Maybe it* was *the HDL. Maybe they had bought a fucking clue on how to not get caught. Taking down a famous Oriceran might be enough.*

Cyrus stood in the corner, his right hand curled tightly around something. "You're a damned fool, Brownstone. A damned fool! You're worse than her in some ways." He gestured toward Nadina.

James pointed his blade at Cyrus. "All I wanted to do was taste some delicious barbeque and check out a friend's new place. I didn't bring this shit on you, and you're only not dead because I might need to ask you some questions. You're obviously not the brains behind this shit if someone else is paying you."

Cyrus raised his arm and let out a giggle.

"Are you fucking losing it?" James rumbled.

"You think you're the only one ever to run into serious

trouble? You think you're the only one with special toys?" Cyrus opened his hand. A purple glass bead rested in his palm. "This is a little something I picked up years ago. Something I saved in case I ever ended up in trouble with something I couldn't take out. Kind of my last resort. Seems kind of appropriate to use it now." He gripped it in his fingers and cocked back his arm. "Now, here's how this shit is going to go, Brownstone. You're going to get out of the armor, I'm going to tie you up with Nadina, and I'm going to leave. If you try to stop me, you're going to feel the power of this little baby, and I'll go down as the man who killed James Brownstone."

*Accept attack for possible adaptation,* Whispy sent.

James grunted.

*Not like I was planning on running away,* he thought. *I doubt this fucker can hurt me.*

"Whatever." James shrugged and charged Cyrus.

The traitorous security chief yelled and threw the pebble. It struck James when he was only a yard away. A bright purple flash blinded James, and a cloud of violet-black particles shot from the impact site.

The force of the blast sent James back, and he smashed through the wall with a grunt. Pain suffused his chest.

James sat up on one knee. His armor was pitted, with deep holes reaching the skin underneath in many cases.

*Yessss,* Whispy sent. *Adaptation in progress. Excellent. Moderate damage. Regeneration in progress. Primary combat efficiency unimpeded. Engage target for additional potential adaptation.*

*Pretty sure he doesn't have another one,* James responded.

James grimaced and climbed through the hole in the

wall. Cyrus had managed to actually hurt him, which was impressive, but he hadn't finished James, which meant it was his turn to respond.

"Well, fuck," James rumbled as he looked at Cyrus. "I still had questions for him."

The security chief was slumped against the wall with deep burns all over the front of his body, his eyes open in a death stare and his chest unmoving.

"Shit!" James spun toward Nadina.

She lay on her side, still tied to the chair, struggling against her bonds. Her green uniform was dotted with scorch marks and holes, but she didn't appear to be seriously injured.

*Huh. Those anti-magic emitters saved her life. Funny how that shit worked out.*

They had also been knocked over, and there were streams of dark smoke rising from them.

James hurried over to slice through the ropes with his claws.

Nadina stood, wobbling for a few seconds before yanking the gag out of her mouth and tossing it to the ground. "Are you okay, James?" She frowned as she eyed his armor.

James nodded. The pain had significantly lessened, and most of the holes in his armor were partially sealed. "I'm fine." He marched over to Cyrus' body and ripped into his pocket with his claws.

Nadina's expression turned disgusted. "What are you doing?"

James found Cyrus' phone. It was a little scorched around the edges, but it still was on and had bars. He stood and returned to Nadina, holding out the phone. "My phone's in my truck if you prefer to use that one. Go ahead and call the cops. They're probably swarming around my hotel still."

Nadina glanced at Cyrus and sighed. "It's pathetic, really. This was all so unnecessary."

"What? Him taking me on? Yeah." James shrugged. "Desperate times and shit."

Nadina shook her head. "No, his betrayal. He didn't reveal who he was working for, but he made it very clear this wasn't part of an ideological crusade. He did it simply for the money. He even admitted it wasn't that I paid him poorly, and now look, he's lost his life. What a waste."

"We all get what's coming to us in the end."

James was faintly surprised by Nadina's calm reaction. He had to remind himself that just because she looked young didn't mean she was. She had lived more than twice as long as he had, and even if she hadn't been a bounty hunter, that left plenty of decades to experience the darkness and greed of multiple species. Oriceran was many things, but it was not a peaceful utopia.

He motioned to the hall. "Let's get the hell out of here. My infomancer can hack his phone, and maybe we can figure out who he was working for from that."

Nadina chuckled as she followed him. "I don't think most of my friends in the barbeque community could have rescued me from a group of heavily-armed thugs. You truly are a man of multiple talents."

James snickered as they headed down the hall to the main warehouse floor, but then he heard something clanking outside the loading bay door.

*What the hell is that?*

James threw up a hand and nodded to the corridor. "Something's wrong. You should hide. I don't think it's over."

Nadina lifted her chin, a haughty pride he hadn't seen before on her face. "I'm a Light Elf. I'm not completely defenseless. They don't have their anti-magic toys in the entire pl—"

A huge explosion blew a hole in the loading bay door, littering the ground with smoking bits of aluminum shrapnel.

"Fuck," James rumbled. "This shit just never ends."

# CHAPTER TWENTY-TWO

Three suits of power armor marched through the hole, one with a heavy machine gun, another with a railgun, and a third with a rotary rocket launcher and a large silver blade crackling with blue-white energy.

James grunted. "Are you an elf who can take on power armor? Just do some invisibility shit, go to the truck, and let me do my thing. You might be a great pitmaster, but I'm a great pitmaster *and* ass-kicker. Multiple talents, remember?"

Nadina laughed and backed into the hall. "We should really open a restaurant together, James. It would be glorious."

"I'm good with one." James shrugged. "My keys are in the truck. You can drive away while I'm taking them on."

Nadina shook her head. "I'm not running. I have faith in you." She raised her hands, half-closing her eyes. Her incantations came out as layered melodies, and she vanished.

*Low probability of adaptation potential,* Whispy reported, but *non-zero. Engage and kill enemies.*

The comments were tinged with hope.

James snickered.

*This is the most fun you've had in a couple of years,* he sent.

*Adaptation strengthens host. Mutually beneficial.*

The men in power armor had ceased their advance, but they aimed their weapons at James.

James growled. "I'm starting to get kind of pissy." He gestured toward the dead bodies. "And as you can see, when I get pissy, people die. I don't know what all this is about, but as far as I can see, it involves you fucking with barbeque, which makes me extra angry."

"Then we agree on something very important." A white-haired man stepped through the smoking hole in the loading bay door. He waved his hand to get some of the smoke out of his face.

James stared for a few seconds, having trouble understanding what he was seeing. "Wait, aren't you Atticus Taylor?"

The man nodded. "Indeed, I am, Mr. Brownstone. Indeed, I am. I'm pleased you recognize me." He smiled. "I have to say I've always been a big fan. We've not met before. I don't compete in the same places you do, but you're an inspiration to both the world of barbeque and just simple law and order." He laughed. "Everyone always says you're retired, but then..." He gestured to James. "Well, I never thought I'd be able to see the famous magic armor up close. It's even more impressive in person."

The armored suits spread out slightly.

James grunted and ignored another death request from

Whispy. "You're not getting a fucking autograph after all this shit. What's this even about? I thought it didn't have anything to do with the HDL, but was I wrong?"

"The HDL?" Atticus grimaced. "Those whiny, short-sighted idiots?" He snorted. "Of course not. They were useful patsies, although this whole thing ended up far more expensive than I'd planned. Mercenaries, bribes, blah, blah, blah." He shook his head. "It sounded so cool in my head when I thought about everything, but the expenses just kept piling up." He sighed. "Oh, well. That's business for you."

"I don't get it," James replied. "If this isn't about HDL, why did you do all this? You New Veil?"

Atticus flinched as if struck. "Don't ever associate with me those psychotic murderers. And let me make it clear: I've got nothing against magic or Oricerans. I don't give two shits about politics or Oricerans, other than how they affect my business."

"You just ranted about how you had to spend a ton of money to fuck over Nadina." James glanced down the hall-way, wondering if she was there or if she had taken his advice and gone for the truck. "I don't get it."

"I didn't spend all this money because I'm a bigot. I spent all this money because I have a lot more money on the line." Atticus sighed. "I'm a wealthy man, Mr. Brown-stone. I was before I started my first restaurant. I'm wealthy because I'm smart and take my opportunities. I've slowly expanded my restaurant presence, developed a brand, and reached out to partners. Come on, we both know barbeque chains are a hard thing to spread out compared to burger joints. But I put in my work, slowly and steadily, and then Little Miss Hot Elf shows up in town." He snorted. "She got famous originally because she won a damned reality tv show."

James snorted. "I saw your weak-ass interview. Nadina opening up one place isn't gonna destroy your business."

"Yes, it will." Atticus sighed. "You don't understand because you've only got one place, but my effort was finally coming to fruition. Being wealthy and being able to afford a nationwide rollout are two different things. I've got investors lined up who are going to help expand my restaurants under a franchise model into every damned state within five years. We're talking hundreds of restaurants, and probably a thousand within ten years. Barbeque will become synonymous with Atticus Taylor. With *me!*"

"I still don't get what any of that shit has to do with Nadina."

Atticus curled his hands into fists. "She sashays in here, and suddenly my investors are talking about how she's taking up all the oxygen. If I can't even be the top place in Denver, how the hell are we supposed to take us nationwide? That sort of thing." He scoffed. "I've been working on this deal for the last two years, and they suddenly have cold feet? They even knew she was opening a place, and they didn't care, but when she actually announced the opening date a few months ago, they said they wanted to table the deal for a year and see what happened." He gritted his teeth. "That was not acceptable!"

*Intelligence collection sufficient,* Whispy suggested. *Terminate enemy.*

*I'm trying to give Nadina time to get away. If I fight those armored suits and she's nearby, she could get hurt.*

James didn't move. The power-armored mercs still had their weapons trained on him.

"So this was all because of some big business deal?" James laughed. "Seriously?"

"Not just a big business deal, a deal that would make a lot of money and secure my position in the barbeque and restaurant communities." Atticus pointed at James. "Competitions aren't everything, you know." He sniffed disdainfully. "Yeah, so what if I'm not as dynamic or whatever in my saucing as a lot of people? People like my fucking food and recipes, and that's what's important."

James shrugged. "Not disagreeing."

He almost laughed. There was something absurd about him in extended advanced mode facing off against three armored mercs while a man ranted about barbeque.

After a few seconds, James changed his mind. He was going to have to kick the man's ass, but a guy causing trouble over barbeque was at least something he could relate to. It was better than dealing with the Vax or a weird interplanetary cabal.

"One thing I don't get is why you even care about this business deal," James explained. "You have money. Why do you need more? How rich do you need to be?"

"I'm a millionaire, but this is my chance to become a billionaire," Atticus explained. "It will secure my legacy. Besides, it'll prove to everyone that they have to respect me." He sighed and shook his head. "Look, Brownstone, you're a businessman, and you're a barbeque lover. You've got more in common with me than you do her. We can make a deal."

"Why should I make a deal with you?" James asked.

"Because even if you don't care about having a nation-wide chain, it's only a matter of time before she opens a place near you. You think your restaurant will survive because you're famous?" Atticus scoffed. "No offense, Brownstone, but even when you're not—" he gestured to the armor, "wearing weird magic armor, you're just not, um—let's say you're not a conventionally attractive man. Let's be honest, Mr. Brownstone. You're kind of ugly."

James shrugged. "I'm married. The only person I have to impress is my wife."

Atticus chuckled. "The point is, you and me? We're both human, and neither of us is exactly Jericho Cartwright. All we have is our food to define our image, and it's not enough to be at the top, not anymore. Maybe not ever. Nadina's not just some hot blonde chick in a dress, she's a hot blonde chick who will remain hot for centuries. We'll be moldy in our graves before she gets a wrinkle. I don't care how society changes. Sex appeal sells."

"She's got good food." James shrugged.

"Not saying she doesn't. I'm just saying she's got the total package." Atticus pointed behind him. "And if she wants to, she can gain control of it all—unless we stop her."

*Well,* you *maybe, but you don't need to know that.*

"I'm not having my potential future as a billionaire derailed by her," Atticus continued. "And even if you don't care about money, you should care about your place closing down. She'll destroy you."

James shook his head. "Not if the taste is there."

Atticus scoffed. "This isn't just about the best taste. Come on. We can work a deal. I get that you already have money, but do you have access to investors?" His eyebrows lifted. "Think about that. You don't have to do any of the work, but your recipes? Maybe they join up with mine, and everybody gets to taste what James Brownstone's barbeque is like. Does that sound appealing? Don't you want your tastes to go nationwide?"

"You're pretty fucking dumb if you think you can bribe me." James grunted. "This is simple. You're gonna surrender and I'm going to call the cops, and you're gonna confess to all the shit you did. And then you're going to jail."

Atticus glared at James. "Fine. I gave you your chance." He pointed toward James and nodded to the mercs. "Kill him."

The suit with the railgun opened up first, the roar of the weapon rattling the room. The round struck James, and he jerked back but didn't fall over.

*Eliminate non-melee opponents for maximum efficiency,* Whispy suggested. *Maximum adaptation already achieved against attack type.*

The machine-gunner opened up, long shell casings cascading to the ground like a waterfall of brass. The bullets peppered James, bouncing off his armor with little damage.

Atticus grimaced and slapped his hands to his ears as he backed toward the hole.

*Don't like what it means to be around a real fight, huh?*

A rocket exploded around James. With a loud click, the rotary launcher spun and readied the next projectile.

James ran toward the machine-gunner. Even though that enemy represented the least direct threat, the constant stream was annoying.

The enemy's partner recharged his railgun and fired another round. The attack missed James and blasted through several walls, exiting the back of the warehouse and sending up a cloud of wood, drywall chunks, and dust.

James stabbed through the center of the machine gunner's armor and pushed until the bloodied blade emerged from the other side. "Yeah, wouldn't have helped even if you'd had magic on this thing."

Atticus yelped and ran outside.

Everyone underestimated his blade. There were few things it couldn't cut with sampling, and reinforced Earth alloys without any magical enhancement might as well have been cardboard.

With a growl, James yanked the blade out, and the armored merc fell to the floor with a loud clank. A rocket smashed into his side. The flames surrounded him for a second.

James crouched and leapt toward the railgunner this time, and both men fell to the ground in a tangle of armored limbs. Three quick stabs into the armor, and it stopped moving. When James removed his blade, blood dripped to the ground.

The remaining enemy lowered the rocket launcher and lifted the sword.

*Yesss,* Whispy sent. *Potential adaptation potential.*

James might not care all that much about adaptation anymore, but Whispy might as well enjoy the outing. Cyrus had actually managed to attack James with a new type of weapon, so maybe the armor could as well. With a roar, James sprinted toward the remaining enemy.

The armored merc brought down the energy-infused

sword, and it bounced off James' shoulder with a loud clang.

*Maximum adaptation already achieved against existing attack type,* Whispy reported. *Eliminate enemy.*

James' momentum helped with that as he shoved the blade deep into the center of the suit and cut up, almost slicing his opponent in half. The merc fell to the ground, and a pool of blood started forming beneath him.

*Just some fancy normal sword, then, huh?* James thought.

*Previous adaptation in battle sequence sufficient to justify engagement,* Whispy suggested.

*Is that your way of saying you're satisfied with what you got? Fine by me. We're not done yet, though.*

James jogged toward the destroyed loading bay door. There was a distant, dull roar in the distance. There was no way Atticus was escaping, but the pitmaster skidded to a halt once he stepped outside and looked around.

Atticus was only a few yards from the hole.

The man lay off to the side, bound in rope and gagged. A smug-looking Nadina stood above him with a grin, her arms folded.

James glanced between Atticus and Nadina and retracted his helmet. "You were supposed to get out of here."

Nadina shook her head. "I might have underestimated you. I was worried those machines might have been able to hurt you, so I stuck around in case I needed to help you escape with a spell." She reached into the pocket of her uniform and pulled out Cyrus' phone. "And sticking around helped anyway. I recorded the entire conversation using my traitorous security chief's phone. I'm not sure if that was clever or just sad, but at least it'll make the police's job easier. They should be here soon."

"Where did you get the rope?" James pointed his blade at Atticus.

Nadina pointed to herself. "I appreciate how you always think of me as a pitmaster first and an elf second, but a simple entanglement spell is something a half-trained elf child can pull off."

"True enough." James grunted. "I've seen Alison do them." He shrugged. "You're right, I do just think of you as a pitmaster. I always have."

James looked in the direction of the dull roar. A gray-black form approached in the sky.

"Huh. I think that's an AET dropship. Whatever you told them must have sounded convincing."

Nadina laughed. "I told them the truth. James Brownstone was taking on an army."

James crouched by Atticus. "You're a dumb asshole. You should have just been satisfied with what you had, because I doubt your investors are going to give you any money now."

Atticus glared back, his curses obvious even behind the gag.

James stood and smiled. He might have had to run around Denver killing people, but the barbeque he'd eaten the other day had been great, and even Whispy had gotten a little treat. Sometimes exercise could be refreshing.

*Huh. This shit was fun.*

## CHAPTER TWENTY-THREE

That evening, James sat across from Nadina in a booth at her restaurant. The place was somehow even more packed than the first night. Atticus' kidnapping attempt had ironically been good advertising for the Spice and Spell. None of her private security was present since they were still sorting out who could be trusted, but a small number of Denver police officers had been stationed there.

James took a deep breath as he raised his fork, his stomach churning. He didn't mind helping Nadina, but she'd just asked him to do something that went against his very nature.

Nadina watched him with a disarming smile. "It won't kill you."

James closed his eyes and shoved the tofu into his mouth. He chewed a few times before grimacing. "It might kill me. I'm sorry. I'll just never be into this."

Nadina laughed. "Oh, James. Your wife must be a saint to tolerate your eccentricities."

"She's patient in her own way," James responded after swallowing some beer to get the tofu out of his mouth. He picked up a rib and took a few bites. He needed meat to get the taste out.

Nadina looked around the packed restaurant. "People are surprised I'm here today. A few people have commented on that."

"You got kidnapped. Most people don't go back to work right away after something like that." James shrugged. "I'm kind of surprised too."

"I think it's extra-important for me to do just that, though. To show I can't be intimidated." Nadina sighed. "This whole thing turned out to be a business rival, but next time it might be the HDL, and you might not be around. I'm going to have to take security far more seriously than I have in the past."

James nodded and set his rib down. "Meaning what? No more charity events?"

Nadina shook her head. "No. I'm just acknowledging that my love of barbeque might not be enough to win over some of my critics." She stared at him for a moment. "I don't suppose there's any chance you would agree to be my new chief of security? I'd pay you well."

James snickered. "No damned way. I'm good when it comes to pointing me at someone to beat down, but I don't like the other parts. If you're ever in Seattle and need extra help, you can look up my daughter, but she wouldn't want to work directly for you either. We Brownstones…kind of need to do our own thing."

"Understood. I had to ask, but I was serious about opening a restaurant with you." Nadina smiled.

"I'm fine with my one place. It'll be a long time before I can handle multiple restaurants."

"I'm going to live a long time," Nadina replied. "I can wait."

James glanced at a happy couple enjoying their brisket. "You know what I don't get?"

"What?" Nadina looked curious.

"I looked up the reviews for Atticus Taylor's restaurants. A lot of them aren't even that good. Everyone says he's more about schtick than cooking, and everything's overpriced for the quality." James frowned. "I barely know anything about the guy because I haven't eaten at any of his places and he's not big in the competition scene."

Nadina nodded. "Is it really so shocking that someone could expand with substandard food? Let's be honest, James: most chains are mediocre at best. They're pushing familiarity and standardization, not the true soul of food, barbeque or otherwise. I might pity a man who wanted to be associated with mediocrity, but I'm not surprised by him."

"You can expand without being a chain," James commented. "You don't have a chain. Each restaurant is different, from the menu to the building."

"Of course. To me, Oriceran fusion barbeque means understanding how to combine what I like with the flavors best suited to each region." Nadina inhaled deeply. "That's what I love about this planet and humans. There's so much diversity for a single species. We have a variety of species on Oriceran, but the simple reality is if you're a Light Elf, you're far more likely to be like another Light Elf than a human is to another human, depending on what country they live in. That's one of the reasons Earth is so special."

"I hadn't really thought a lot about that. I like what I like. Other people like what they like. Even if it's tofu." James made a face.

Nadina folded her hands in front of her, a curious glint in her eye. "If you're not going to open another restaurant soon, are you sure you'll be satisfied?"

"Why wouldn't I be?"

"I don't know. I might be projecting too much of myself onto you. When I started my first restaurant, I didn't have the intention of starting an empire, but I found myself dissatisfied after a while. We elves are supposed to be far more patient than humans, but in this case, I'm more a like a human child. I always want to move onto the next big thing."

James forked some brisket onto his plate before shaking his head. "I've had my place for eight years now. It's small, mostly takeout, and it doesn't make me anywhere near the money bounty hunting does, but I wouldn't have it any other way. Besides, the last thing I should be doing is worrying about another restaurant when I've got a new kid coming soon."

Nadina's breath caught. "Your wife is pregnant?"

James nodded. "Yeah. Not that far along."

"Congratulations." Nadina smiled warmly. "Children are lovely."

"What about you?" James asked. "You ever think about having kids? Or do you already have some?"

"No, not at all." Nadina tilted her head and looked into the distance before giving a shallow nod. "I'm still young, which is why I can indulge my whims with things such as running barbeque restaurants, but yes, I do intend to have some when the time is right."

James chuckled. "I don't know if the time is ever right. I didn't think I was ready with Alison, and at first, I didn't think I was ready for this new kid, but it is what it is. You never know what is going to happen."

"I suppose that's true." Nadina smiled. "If you had asked me when I was younger if elves would ever walk openly on Earth, I would have thought it was insanity."

James nodded. "So, if you're young, what would be a good age to start having kids?"

Nadina furrowed her brow. "I don't know. Maybe in fifty or sixty years."

James picked up his half-empty beer bottle and chuckled. "Well, tonight, let's just finish our barbeque. It's been fun, but I'm heading back home tomorrow."

"I know I've said it before, but let me say it again." Nadina reached over and patted his hand. "Thank you for everything you've done. The police are taking my protection seriously, so I have no concerns until I get my security situation well in hand. You're a good friend. You have gone above and beyond."

"Sure, but like I told a lot of these guys, they shouldn't have fucked with barbeque," James growled.

Nadina smiled. "Then I'll endeavor never to betray barbeque."

# CHAPTER TWENTY-FOUR

James settled into his recliner, a sleeping Thomas curled up beside the chair. It was good to be back home. The trip back from Denver had been free of bounties, business rivals, moronic carjackers, or anything other than good food. He'd hit a few different barbeque places along the way, appreciating their focus.

Atticus had lawyered up, but Nadina's recording meant he didn't have a chance. The authorities believed James wouldn't even have to testify, but he'd make the time if it was needed.

Shay yawned as she emerged from the kitchen with a pint of Blue Bell ice cream and a huge spoon in hand. "I don't know if it's supposed to be too early, but I've already got this fucking super-obsession with strawberry ice cream." She pointed the spoon at James. "Maybe I'll send you on an ice cream road trip next time. You can find some super-rare strawberry ice cream for me."

"Wouldn't it melt?" James asked with a curious expression.

Shay rolled her eyes. "You once spent several days fleeing hitmen with a cooler full of ribs. I'm sure you can find a way to keep my ice cream cold." She dropped onto the couch and dug into the ice cream. "Just keep in mind that next time, it won't all be ass-kicking and barbeque."

James grunted. "I'll remember that, but I don't think I'll need to take a road trip for a while."

Shay swallowed the bite of ice cream. "Oh?"

"Yeah. Everything's fine now. I got my head screwed on straight about the kid and my future. You, the kid, and a single restaurant." James put up his footrest. "No empires, no expanding all over the place, no weird-ass grilled tofu barbeque."

"Grilled tofu?" Shay raised an eyebrow. "You ate grilled tofu barbeque?"

"Nadina gave me some." James shuddered at the memory. "She wanted me to try some 'eggplant steaks' as well, but I refused on that one."

"She's far braver than I thought." Shay set her ice cream carton in her lap. "And you're seriously okay? The whole point of sending you on the trip was so you could relax, but you helped Trey take down that bastard in Vegas, fought a bunch of enhanced wizards, got carjacked, and battled half a mercenary company, it sounds like."

James frowned. "I didn't get carjacked."

"Okay, you were subjected to an 'attempted carjacking.'" Shay made air quotes around the last two words. "I know that kind of thing isn't a danger to you, but I was just worried that it might be annoying, is all."

James shook his head. "Nah. The whole point of the trip was to eat good barbeque, and I did have plenty of that in-between, even if a lot of shit came up. It wasn't a big deal. It wasn't as bad as in Chile."

Shay eyed him with suspicion. "You could always do more, you know."

"What are you talking about? I told you already I'm fine with one restaurant."

"Not the restaurant." Shay sighed. "Bounty hunting. It's not like you have to restrict yourself to shit that comes up incidentally while you're wandering around. If you miss it, you could start purposely going after high-level bounties. Bounty-hunting road trips?"

James thought that over for a few seconds before shaking his head. "But I don't really miss it. I don't mind kicking ass when I need to, but this shit with Nadina and all the investigation stuff is annoying, even when I'm not having to deal with Davion."

"Okay. As long as you're happy, I'm happy." Shay smiled. "I'm the same. I don't mind the occasional tomb raid, but I don't miss doing them constantly, and I honestly thought I would. I thought I needed the danger, but I don't."

James let out a long, contented sigh. "Yeah, I got everything out of my system, and having Nadina's barbeque only reminded me of what I like about mine. I'm happy to have a kid coming. I'm happy with my daughter, and I'm happy with my life."

"Good." Shay stood and walked toward the kitchen. "Next time, maybe don't use so many artifacts. I'd go and grab a few of my own, but I'll have Lily do it instead, just to be on the safe side." She grabbed the lid for the ice cream from the counter and put in on before opening the freezer. "I'm happy, too. Maybe it's not a big surprise, but not constantly risking my life or having strange magical foes try to kill me has actually been pretty damned satisfying."

James grunted. "Yeah, it is. I'm ready to go back to my own place and just have a relaxing time cooking barbeque."

Shay poked her head around the refrigerator to grin at James. "You haven't worked through the implications, have you?"

James frowned. "What implications?"

"You just saved a celebrity chef," Shay explained, her grin growing wider. "One of the most celebrated chefs in the country, or pitmaster, whatever you want to call her. You saved her from a high-profile kidnapping. You see, the media's gotten used to dealing with you. They know they can't call you and have you talk, especially after that little interview in Denver."

James frowned. "Meaning what?"

Shay looked far too happy. "I bet there's an army of reporters watching your restaurant. The minute you arrive, they are going to swarm you like hungry locusts."

James scrubbed a hand over his face. "Shit. Maybe I'll take a few more days off."

# AUTHOR NOTES

## MAY 30, 2019

**THANK YOU for not only reading this story but these *Author Notes* as well.**

(I think I've been good with always opening with "thank you." If not, I need to edit the other *Author Notes*!)

### RANDOM (*sometimes*) THOUGHTS?

I think I find the *thought* of talking to a lot of people more romantic (or businesslike) than the reality of actually talking to a lot of people.

I enjoy talking, but I find it a bit energy-sapping when I talk to people, especially strangers, non-stop. It isn't that I don't like people. Far from it. It's just mentally taxing, or perhaps emotionally taxing might be a better description.

That could be why I like reading so much. I get to enjoy talking and communication (if vicariously watching it happen between characters) without the energy suckage.

I understand there are others who get energized when they are talking to people. I'm the guy who doesn't understand that. I enjoy working on creative problems with people, for sure. I'm also the person who (after a long week at the 20Booksto50k(™) conference) just wants to hide and write.

Are you that way? Do you find constant interaction with others energy-creating or energy-reducing (or neither)?

I think I baked this desire for solitude into the character of James Brownstone. It's often said that our first main character (Bethany Anne for me) is a reflection of us, or perhaps the person we want to be.

(I'd be good with having her power and money, not so much her fetish for shoes and clothes (that's my wife.))

Now, with Brownstone, I'll admit to writing in my KISS preference and BBQ love (yes to sauce. Dry rub is nice, but there better be some sauce with it. No to vinegar-based sauce as well. I come from Texas, so tomato-based sauce is my preference. If you want to argue this, do it in a short story ;-). )

I'm not a dog lover (they are fun, but I don't want to have one) like Brownstone, and I enjoy cats when someone else has to deal with them and their "better than you" attitude.

But, if I had to choose, I'd probably go with a...*damn*... I'm thinking cat, but probably would go with a dog. At least the dog would give me love and affection when I'm ready for it. A cat would probably figure out how to give me the finger when I want to pet it. and I've had a cat climb up my leg before.

I probably still have the scars from the claws.

## AROUND THE WORLD IN 80 DAYS

One of the interesting (at least to me) aspects of my life is the ability to work from anywhere and at any time. In the future, I hope to re-read my own *Author Notes* and remember my life as a diary entry.

**Somewhere in the sky between Dallas and New York**. Off to Book Expo, New York for a fun week of talking to people and meetings! Lots and lots of meetings.

A lot of them.

*Damn.*

The people are great (the ones I already know), and I'm happy to meet them again. The business is solid, and we are growing our backlist, producing our own audio (and selling the rights to many more), and looking to acquire software to help us manage our production capabilities.

But it just requires sooo many meetings ;-)

(Yes, all of these meetings, should they be at lunch or dinner, are tax write-offs. At least something good comes out of it.)

However, I wouldn't trade any of it for a quieter life.

*I'm living the dream.*

**FAN PRICING**

$0.99 Saturdays (new LMBPN stuff) and $0.99 Wednesday (both LMBPN books and friends of LMBPN books.) Get great stuff from us and others at tantalizing prices.

Go ahead. I bet you can't read just one.

Sign up here: http://lmbpn.com/email/.

**HOW TO MARKET FOR BOOKS YOU LOVE**

Review them so others have your thoughts, and tell friends and the dogs of your enemies (because who wants to talk to enemies?)... *Enough said ;-)*

Ad Aeternitatem,

Michael Anderle

# CONNECT WITH MICHAEL ANDERLE

**Michael Anderle Social**
   **Website:**
   http://www.lmbpn.com

**Email List:**
   http://lmbpn.com/email/

**Facebook Here:**
   https://www.facebook.com/OriceranUniverse/
   https://www.
facebook.com/TheKurtherianGambitBooks/